TO TOUCH THE LIGHT

An Irons and Works Holiday Novel

E.M. LINDSEY

To Touch the Light
E.M. Lindsey

Cover Design by Amai Designs

Dear Readers,

I just wanted to take a moment to express my thanks for taking a risk on a holiday book that doesn't encompass the traditional Christmas storyline. Often, other holidays are forgotten in a sea of lit trees and Santa and winter wonderlands. Chanukah is not 'Jewish Christmas'—it is a minor holiday, but one with a lot of purpose and meaning. I hope that you can take away the same sort of joy from this book—and the love the men find in it—as you can any other holiday romance.

I want to take a moment to say that this book contains a main character who is a transgender man. He uses specific terms to refer to his anatomy, like 'dick', which may or may not be the same way other transgender men refer to their body. His experience is not meant to represent all transgender men, and please take care to remember existing as transgender is and always will be a profoundly personal experience for each individual. All the same, with the help of sensitivity readers, I hope to have done him justice.

Please be aware that this story does contain mentions of anxiety and dysphoria, so if these are triggering issues for you, feel free to skip this book.

As always, I hope you enjoy reading this as much as I enjoyed writing it.

All my love,
Elaine

Let him kiss me with the kisses of his mouth, for your love is better than wine.

King Solomon, Song of Songs 1:2

Chapter 1

"I want this place cleaned. Spotless. I don't have time to worry whether or not you're keeping up on your goddamn side-work." Mario's voice rang through the kitchen, the handful of line cooks staring at him with the usual fear in their eyes. He didn't hate it. He worked hard for his reputation as the Devil of Fairfield Resort in a world that didn't want men like him in charge of anything.

"*Yes, Chef!*"

The echoed cry was almost comical in a way—the fuckers behind his line watched too many episodes of Kitchen Whatever with furious, red-faced British men stomping around in their whites and non-slip kicks. Some of it reflected what his life was like—the long hours, constant complaints, customers with unrealistic demands, people who just couldn't fucking keep it together on the line no matter how hard he rode their asses. And he wasn't a nice guy. He hadn't gotten to where he was by being a nice guy.

He fought his way to the top, standing with his shoulders back and head high when they inevitably learned he was a trans man and they went from respecting him to looking at him like he was some girl playing dress-up in his daddy's clothes. It was the same everywhere he went, but at Fairfield Resort, Mario Garcia had reputation. It was carefully cultivated and, even if he did get tired of being a raging asshole all the time, he couldn't afford to let his mask slip. Not once.

That would lead to disaster—to a coup in his kitchen—to some cis-gender little upstart with too much ego trying to take over. He could set his watch by that cycle, and he was tired of it.

Glancing around the kitchen, he saw it was in the best shape it would be before the dinner rush. He was off that night—the hotel barely at fifteen percent capacity, which meant he could afford the time away. He could hand the spatula and apron over to his sous, Cash, and not worry about shit getting done.

A night like tonight, he'd only get a couple of crisis calls, and he could live with that. He rubbed his hand down his sternum, an absent gesture until he realized he was doing it. His meeting with his F&B manager was in twenty minutes, then just enough time to shower, to shave, to head down to the little tattoo shop where he was taking one of many steps to reclaiming and loving his body as his own.

"I'll be upstairs in Joanne's office if anyone needs me. But don't need me. Heard?"

"Heard," came the echo, far less enthusiastic than, "*Yes, Chef*," and that, he could deal with.

Mario paused in his office to grab his bag, not bothering to change since he hated how starchy the laundry staff got his uniform, then grabbed his keys and phone and stepped into the hall. He had his back to the wall, locking the door, when something slammed into his legs.

"What the fuck? *God* can't you," his words died on his tongue at the sight of his favorite dishwasher. Which, really, was an absurd thing to say about a person—but he really did like the guy.

Viktor. He was an immigrant from Russia or Siberia or something—he wasn't sure since the guy barely spoke English and rarely talked to anyone. But he was a hard worker, always kept his head down, always did what was expected of him.

There was more to it though, more to *him*. Mario knew it—he recognized a kindred spirit a little too easily these days. Viktor was a sort of man with a secret. Maybe not one that mirrored his own, but he knew all too well what it looked like when you kept things close to your chest.

His only real issue with the guy was his eyesight. The poor man was severely myopic. He couldn't read for shit, and couldn't see ten feet in front of him, which was likely why Mario was sporting a bruise on the side of his ankle.

"Jesus, Viktor, where's the fire?"

Viktor cleared his throat and looked up with those unfocused, maple-colored doe eyes that Mario tried to ignore because they made his heart race. "Fire? There's *fire*...?"

"No, god." Mario tried not to smile because it was irritatingly cute, and a man of Viktor's age—with his slightly greying curls and crow's feet—should not be cute. "It's a metaphor. You know, like a figure of speech. It means where are you going in such a rush?"

"Ah." Viktor rubbed the back of his neck and shrugged before gripping the cart. "Darla—in bar. Wanting glasses. Want me to hurry."

"I shouldn't keep you," Mario said, waving his hand. "But hey," he called after him, and his stomach fluttered when Viktor paused in his step. "Be careful, okay? I don't want you getting hurt."

Viktor looked back over his shoulder, wearing a smile which made Mario feel hot all over. "Yes, *solnyshko*. Always." He wasn't sure Viktor could see him, but he watched as the other man nodded, then returned to his route, not slowing his pace at all.

"*Idiot*," Mario muttered, but it was with a fondness he didn't feel for anyone else who worked for him. He felt an irrational desire to protect Viktor from the cruelty that could be working in a kitchen. He did his job well, but he seemed so out of place in the bowels of the resort. He belonged outside where he could be in the sun, where the light could touch him.

This place was a pit, and Mario's gut twisted to see Viktor condemned to it.

All the same, he didn't have time to contemplate the fates of the people working for him. His own life was busy enough, chaotic enough, and he didn't have the energy to fix anyone else. With a sigh, he turned toward the staff elevator and made his way up to the executive offices. Joanne was in her office, leaning back in her desk chair with her cell phone pressed to her ear by her shoulder. She was clicking around on her keyboard, and waved him to a seat as she finished up her conversation.

"Yes. *No*...I want *geese*. Because it's fucking Christmas and that's a thing. I'm not going to ruin this because you want to save cash with duck. Don't fight me. I'm trying to look like I give a shit here. This is...yes. Yes. No."

She ended the call without ceremony. If Mario hadn't been working for her for the last several years, it might have startled him, but he was used to the abrupt way she handled her business.

"Okay, so, I have exactly twelve minutes before I have

to be out the door," she told him, folding her hands on the desk in front of her. "What's the problem?"

Mario took a breath and considered his argument. Joanne liked things a certain way, and the owners gave her leeway to handle events without being kept in check, so it wasn't often he had any cards to pull with her. But he'd overheard two of the servers complaining that when they brought up Chanukah, they'd been dismissed as it not being relevant.

It bothered him, and although he'd always been peripherally aware of other winter holidays, it hadn't occurred to him to do anything about it. Except this year. This year, he wanted to offer something more. He had done this same song and dance over Christmas for years—the same tree, the same lights, the same food. The same fussy older people with big checkbooks and bigger attitudes. He was just tired.

And it might be the same with another group of people, but it was worth the risk. It was worth the risk for the hotel to be a little more inclusive, and it was worth the risk to put his reputation on the line. He just had to get it right, and that's where he worried.

"I want to book the Diamond Room for Sunday," he said.

She blinked at him. "Christmas Eve Eve?"

Mario rolled his eyes. "You and I both know Christmas Eve Eve is not an actual thing. And yes, Sunday, which is the second night of Chanukah, and I'd like to set up a banquet."

Joanna looked at him again, then threw her head back and laughed. "You know, everyone tells me you don't have a sense of humor, but you're actually hilarious."

When her chuckles died down, he laid his hands on the desk and stared at her. "I'm not joking."

"Mario," she breathed out, but he didn't want her to have time to form an argument.

"We already have some people interested in the idea," he went on.

"*Some* people…"

"…and there will be *more* if we advertise it as hard as you've been doing with the Christmas banquet," he finished, ignoring her protest.

She leaned forward, resting her elbow on the desk, her chin on her curled fist, and she stared at him for a long moment of silence. "Coming to me, wanting to throw another holiday banquet five days before the actual holiday is insanity. You know that, right?"

He shrugged. "You think we can't pull it off?"

"I think that it's a waste of time and money, and I'm not going to sign off on something like that. You want to throw some Jew party…"

"Joanne," he hissed at her.

She rolled her eyes. "You want to throw some '*alternative holiday party*'," she said using air quotes, "fine. But do it with the proper amount of time for both budget approval and planning."

"Alright," he said. He waited until she sat back, looking triumphant, then he smiled. "I'll call the rabbi and tell him what you said."

Her cheeks pinked and he felt a rush of satisfaction. "Tell him what, exactly?"

"What you said. About some 'Jew'," he used air quotes, "alternative holiday party not being worth it."

"That's not…"

"I'm sure he'll understand. I'm sure he hears it a lot." He knew he was going over the top, but her bigotry often went unchecked because she made money for the hotel and got things done. But they lived in an age of viral news stories that had no problem coming down on some uppity white woman who wanted to keep her holiday superior.

"You really think you can get this done?" she challenged.

He shrugged. "I won't know until I try."

"And you know how the fuck to put together a *Chanukah* buffet?"

At that, he laughed. "Hell no, I don't. I mean, I've made kosher food before, and I've done plenty of bar and bat mitzvahs. But I have no idea what goes into a Chanukah dinner."

"So, how the hell do you plan to pull this off?" Her eyes were ablaze, and he felt no remorse.

"Winging it and asking people who *do* know." It was as simple as that. Mario had built his reputation, not out of pretending like he knew it all, but knowing when to call in the experts. He had the internet at his disposal—information at the tips of his fingers that was easy enough to use. And he knew people. Plenty who worked in Fairfield. It wasn't an impossible task.

"Bring me an outline of what we need by this evening," she told him.

Mario shook his head. "Tomorrow. I have an appointment tonight I can't miss."

"You're telling me whatever you have is more important than this fucking banquet you just dropped in my lap?" she demanded.

He shrugged, then rubbed at his sternum again, and she didn't miss it. Her cheeks pinked again with discomfort, but he didn't pull back. "That's what I'm telling you. I know you trust me, even if we don't always get along. So, let me handle this, and I promise it will go off without a hitch."

"If it goes up in flames, it's your ass, not mine," she warned him.

Mario rose and shrugged. "I can live with that. Talk to you later." He marched out, letting the door close a little harder than was necessary. He was able to leave the property with his head high, and without a scrap of guilt weighing him down.

Staring at himself in the mirror, Mario took a deep breath in, watching his ribs expand, watching the half-moon scars stretch and deepen. He let the breath out, and he winced at the way his waist still curved in, hour-glassing just above his hips, which had squared off and bulked out a bit with the sheer number of hours he spent at the gym sculpting his abs.

And logically, he knew his body was fine. Logically, he was fit and well put together—but his brain and logic hadn't been friends in a long time. Maybe not ever. He blinked and saw the person he was before he choked out the words, "I'm not a girl," to his mother, who had laughed and patted him on the head and told him, "I was a tomboy just like you, but I got over it."

He spent years as a butch lesbian, shaving his head and gauging his ears and wearing double sports bras that flattened his chest, cutting off his air supply just so he could feel like he could breathe again. He bit his nails short and walked with bowlegs and only owned work boots because they naturally created a stomp regardless of how light his gait was.

At twenty-one, things changed. At twenty-one, his therapist handed him a pamphlet with words that made him cry so hard he couldn't breathe—and kept him up for two nights straight. He spent the next week surviving on coffee and bagel scraps, and working himself so hard he didn't have time to think.

The Monday after, he sat in her office chair and repeated those words he'd uttered at his mother all those years ago. "*I'm not a girl.*"

This time, there was no laughter, no pat on the head. This time there were referrals and more therapy appointments and so much literature he went to bed when his eyes crossed and everything was doubled.

His girlfriend broke up with him when she realized he was serious about it. About the testosterone, and the surgery, and that his name was Mario now—after his great-grandfather who died when he was sixteen, but had taken him on his knee and whispered in old Spanish, "You can be anyone you want to be." Not any*thing*, but any*one*, and he didn't know what that really meant at the time, but now...

If only those realizations and revelations—those moments of looking at himself and saying, "I'm *Mr.* Garcia," and hearing it in a voice several octaves lower than he'd ever spoken before, and staring at his beard he had to wear trimmed because he worked in a kitchen—if only those were enough.

For all intents and purposes, he was one of the most accomplished men in his family. College educated, a job-change because teaching sucked, and he wasn't good at it anyway. He worked his way into a head chef position at the only resort in the Fairfield city limits, and he'd been there ten years now.

So, he was good, really. But sometimes, there was an itch he couldn't scratch. He knew, though, that someday he'd stop feeling like he was choking every time a stranger looked at him with his shirt off. This was step one. This was the start—at least he hoped. Because nothing else was working.

"Hey, man. You all set?"

The voice behind Mario startled him, which was ridiculous since he was at a tattoo appointment for fuck's sake. He turned away from the mirror and offered Mat a tentative smile, dragging one hand through his hair. "Sorry. I haven't slept in like four days and my brain is fucked."

Mat's brow furrowed. "You alright?"

Mario shrugged. He liked that the guys at Irons and Works talked to him like they were friends—and in a way, they were. He'd spent enough money and time in each of their chairs, trying to fill a desperate, aching hole inside himself that would one day be full, and one day allow him to look in the mirror and never again see the ghost of the person he was.

He was getting closer too. He usually only saw glimpses, old shadows. Today was just a bad day, and he knew the stress of it was weighing on him. The holidays were approaching, which meant families were coming into town, and the old Christmas traditions of big turkey dinners were falling by the wayside and more posh, pre fixe meals and decadent pastries at high end restaurants were taking their place.

And it was Mario's job to see that it all went off without a hitch. Their Christmas celebration at Fairfield Resort was growing larger each year. They put on a tree lighting ceremony now, had a snow day for the kids, had a Christmas morning brunch for families. They had a gift exchange and sleigh rides and the works.

His job was to make it look like a winter fantasy—to make it feel as special as anyone's grandma did back when they were kids. Only richer, and prettier.

And he could do that, even if it cost him weeks of real

sleep and at least twenty pounds of stress weight as he ate his feelings in the form of Christmas cookies.

So yeah. He was fine. He just...wasn't *fine*.

He absently ran his thumb over his left scar, feeling a strange, numbing tingle, because the feeling never quite came back the same way, and he lowered himself to the bench where Mat waited with the stencils. These tattoos were a long time coming. He'd done his arms—half-sleeves from shoulder to elbow—one entire calf, the right side of his neck, and one down his spine. But he'd avoided his chest for a long time. Mostly because he never found what looked right, but also because he wasn't ready to let it all go.

He was now.

Maybe.

Probably.

Mat had the stencil on thin paper, a spray bottle next to it, a stick of gel to help apply the ink. The image looked strange without the shading, but he knew Mat's work, he knew it would be perfect. A stag, right in the center of his stomach, and the antlers would cascade up his chest, covering his two scars, bracketing his nipples.

"What do you think?" Mat asked.

Mario licked his lips, then nodded because it was exactly what he wanted. It would mostly be geometric, with some shading, sort of stark but plain—a lot like who he was as a person. There was a lot about him that stood out just by existing. A Latino, trans, gay man who worked as a head chef in a very white little hipster town—it was hard to really blend. But he wasn't a loud personality, or a very enthusiastic one.

He was a dick at work—but all chefs were. If he was soft, nothing got done. He was short with people in his personal life because he had trust issues.

He was a mess at home because he was like a newborn in a way—only just ready to say, *This is me, and I love me. I'm ready, and I'm here, and this is it.*

His point of pride was getting there on his own, but little blips still existed.

Mostly, he knew—a quiet voice that he rarely paid attention to—he just wanted to be loved. Wanted to be wanted. He wanted to not explain himself to dates, only to watch the guy nod and smile and pretend to be cool before his cousin's neighbor's grandma's cat had a life-threatening emergency and bailed on him.

He wanted to not be ghosted for existing in the body he had.

"You know if you need me to make a change, there's still time," Mat told him.

Mario let out a dusty, soft laugh. "Nah, man. It's great."

"You're just quiet," Mat said. He picked up the alcohol spray, then the little disposable razor, and began to clean up the area Mario had already pre-shaved. The blade was annoying and rough, but there was a lot more to come and it would be a lot more than just annoying. "I mean, you're always quiet, but more than usual."

Mario laughed again, good-naturedly because he did like Mat a lot. He liked what the guy had done with himself—that he'd sort of clawed his way out of his own hell and made his life his own. He didn't let the fact that he couldn't read, and sometimes had trouble speaking, control his future. And he got married. He got married and he was happy, and Mario—*god*, he wanted that.

"Are you making fun of me? You know you're not supposed to mock the guy about to jab you repeatedly with a tattoo machine, right?"

Mario rolled his eyes, but he was grinning now and feeling better. "It's the fucking holidays."

Mat blinked at him, then shook his head and took out the little gel stick, swiping it in firm strokes over Mario's extra smooth chest. The hairlessness made him a little twitchy—and he knew why, and he knew it wasn't forever, but he hated the feeling of missing those coarse strands that he'd worked so fucking hard to grow.

"The holidays," Mat repeated. "Like seasonal depression or…"

"The resort is totally booked over that whole week, and I'm losing my mind. I want to do something nice for the holidays, but my line cooks this year…" He trailed off, shaking his head. "The only good ones I got on my team are those kids from Ted House and they're all minors." Which meant they could only work a certain number of hours that week. He wasn't going to be the monster that kept foster kids in a sweaty kitchen on Christmas, either. He was going to be the guy who sent them home with big fat bonuses and a little gift each.

He was Grinchy, he wasn't Satan.

"That sucks, man," Mat told him.

Mario blew out a puff of air. "Yeah. It does. And I had this idea—I wanted to do something with Chanukah too. No one ever does shit, so why not us. But my boss started giving me shit, so I think I just made a bunch of promises I don't know if I can keep. Like marketing this thing, and figuring out a menu with enough time to order everything, and get it cooked. I'm so fucking in over my head."

"What are you going to do?" Mat stuck his tongue between his teeth as he angled the stencil paper over the freshly prepared area, and Mario appreciated how good-looking Mat was. Hell, if it had been a few years ago…

But it was hard to think that way. Mario had also met

Mat's husband several times and couldn't really imagine the two of them loving anyone else.

"I'm going do my damn best. I'm going to research until I can't see straight, and I'm going to scream at my staff and threaten them until they get their heads out of their asses," Mario said dryly.

Mat froze, laughed, then carefully stuck the stencil paper to his chest. He gave it a couple of light taps with the tips of his gloved fingers, then looked up at him with his big, brown eyes. "Does it work when you do that?"

"No. But it makes me feel better when it all goes to hell." Mario held his breath when Mat edged the corner of the paper up, then carefully peeled it away. He tilted his head from right to left, then left to right, then nodded.

"Go check the mirror and if you like it, we can get started."

Mario stood, eyeing the little plastic ink cups filled with various shades of blacks, greys, and whites, and he mentally prepared himself for the vibrating sting that was about to take hours. He turned back to the mirror and forced himself to look only at the stag, only at the way the lines and curves cascaded across his naked skin.

This is the last time I'll look at my chest—blemished and unblemished.

"I love it," he said, and it was more than gratifying to know it wasn't a lie. He walked back to the chair, then adjusted the neck pillow Mat provided, and let his legs relax off to the side. It would have been nice to just sleep, to let himself go, but as high as his pain tolerance was, he couldn't let himself go when Mat was pulling the needles across his skin.

There was a hand on his side—a little too close to his right scar—and he tensed, but Mat didn't pull back. "Is there anything we can do to help?"

It was so very much like Mat to offer, and Mario shrugged. "I'll figure it out. I always do. It's just been… exhausting. It feels like a constant uphill battle." And he was lonely. Lest he forget with everything else going on, he was lonely. He loved being in the shop, but every single one of them had fallen in love, had gotten married, had started families. It ached a little to watch it from afar, knowing he'd never have it so easy.

Mat eased him back down, waiting until he was comfortable, then he poised the machine over the center of his sternum. "Ready?"

Mario nodded, sticking his tongue between his teeth to keep from clenching his jaw and giving himself a migraine. He took a breath, and then another one as the machine whirred to life. Mat dabbed the tip of his gloved finger through a glob of Vaseline, then rubbed it over the stencil. He met Mario's eyes, then gently brought his arm down.

The first swipe of the needles was always the most jarring. Not the most painful, but it was far too easy to forget the burning sting as his skin was punctured and he was marked, until he was back in the chair. He wouldn't adjust to it—he was sensitive as it was, and it was only the fact that it was worth it that he was willing to sit for so damn long. But after a beat, he allowed himself to relax.

"Tell me about your holiday dinner," Mat said.

Mario recognized that the guy was trying to distract him, and he held back a chuckle so his chest didn't move too much. "Christmas is…Christmas, I guess. Have you guys ever come up to the resort for it?"

Mat shook his head. "Nah. Wyatt's not big on crowds, and neither am I. Plus, I was back in school last year, which was kicking my ass. But I think Tony and Kat take Jazzy and some of the kids to see the tree lighting."

Mario let out a small sigh. "They want more and more

every year, and it feels like it's to the exclusion of everything else. It's…it's one damn day. It's here, and then it's gone, but so many people are forgotten. My entire staff is working until two in the morning—like we don't have families who would rather be sitting around opening gifts and enjoying a dinner with each other."

Except that he didn't. He had nothing—no one. If he could have handled the kitchen on his own, he would have. What was the point of making other people suffer if he could bear it? He couldn't though. He was one man, and that was not nearly enough.

"My boss showed her ass earlier when we were talking. She got a little anti-Semitic with me and it just makes me want to do this whole Chanukah thing even more," Mario confessed.

"That's the hating Jewish people thing, right?" came a voice from the partition doorway.

Mario glanced over and saw Miguel—the newest of the artists, who had taken over most of Mat's clients. Mario hadn't worked with him, but he'd seen what he could do and he would, probably soon. "Yeah," he said. "It's like this casual bigotry people think is funny. She thought I was making a damn joke when I bought up the dinner. I had to threaten her with a rabbi I don't even know to get her to back down."

Mat snorted, carefully swiping a paper towel soaked in Green Soap across his skin before moving on. The pain was a lot, but the conversation was distracting, and was more relaxed in the chair than he'd ever been. "So now you have to go find a rabbi?"

Mario groaned, wanting to slap himself in the face, but he didn't dare move. Mat was getting close to his scars now, and he sucked in a breath. "I guess I'd better do something."

"It helps if you curl your toes," Miguel said.

Mario glanced over with a frown. "What?"

"The scars. When you get them inked—it helps when your curl your toes. Mine are real weird—numb in some spots but sensitive in others. When I get my shit worked on, I curl my toes really tight, then release, over and over. I don't know why it helps. My old boss taught me that trick."

It was the first time Mario acknowledged that he was laying here in the chair in the middle of the shop—behind a low partition—for everyone to see. And he didn't care. It was like the first summer after his surgery when he set foot on the beach and his chest was flat. He was scarred up and too skinny from missing his work-outs, but it was a sort of triumph he hadn't felt again.

That was before the second round of self-consciousness had gripped him by the throat, before the whispers started from the people who used to know him and planted seeds of self-deprecation and doubt. He would never regret his choices, but sometimes he regretted how many people knew about them.

Miguel wasn't looking at him the way others did, though. He was watching as Mat carefully etched around the thick skin, the way he blended the blemishes in his flesh to the ink and made it look like something new. Like art. Like part of him that always belonged there. He had so far to go, but he would never resent the journey.

He curled his toes in his boots, squeezing them tight, then let go. It didn't help the pain, but his mind was focused on it enough that he just didn't notice as much. Offering Miguel a small grin, he closed his eyes and just felt the way Mat marked him.

"It helps," he finally said.

Miguel let out a sigh, then he heard him tap the partition wall twice. "Good. I'm about to take off, text me if you need anything."

It was silent after that, until Mat took a short pause and set the machine down. "Want some music while I finish you up, or do you want to keep talking?"

The answer was simple. "Music," because it wouldn't ask questions. It would just let him be. And right now, that's all he needed.

Chapter 2

It was a bad eye day, as Vitya had taken to thinking of them. He woke early that morning, stiff from his endless nights with nothing more than a thick foam pad between him and the floor. But even that was aging, now bowing under his weight so he felt every groove in the hard wood beneath him. He'd long since accepted that he wouldn't have more, or better. He'd long since come to terms with the idea that a comfortable bed in a warm house that belonged to him was a distant memory and wouldn't ever be more than that. Not again.

He was far from home—though it was hard to think of St. Petersburg as home anymore. It was an ocean away—more than a continent. It was a figment of his imagination some days. It had been so long since he'd seen the streets of the city he was raised in, he wasn't sure anymore what was real and what was fantasy.

It wasn't like this, though, he thought as he pushed himself to stand. He blinked against the blur, his vision fading from clear to looking like a fogged window every couple of seconds. It was disorienting, and some days he wondered if maybe he'd be better off just going totally blind. At least it would be consistent.

With a breath, Vitya shuffled across the cold floor, wanting to turn up the heat, but he couldn't afford much during the winter. He saved up enough for thick socks and heavy sweaters—and a snow-jacket he had no business throwing money at, but without it, he wouldn't survive the long treks to the hotel for his early morning shifts.

Winter didn't come as early or last as long here as it did back home. There were comfortable springs and occasional hard freezes. He'd lived through worse—even if, at the time, he'd been better off.

He started the shower, then thought better of it. He had to leave his little apartment in less than twenty-minutes, and he could already tell it was too cold to risk having wet hair. He washed his face instead, then rummaged around for warm trousers and the thickest sweater he had that didn't smell like a bathroom drain.

His body ached, his fingers a little too tight, but he tugged his beanie on his head and found his keys before locking up. It was such an absurd habit—locking his front door. There was nothing worth stealing. Since he'd made it across the country and hunkered down in this little hovel, wasting his life away washing dishes and enduring snide abuse from the kitchen staff, he hadn't been able to afford much. A roof over his head and a single meal at home per day were his luxuries. How far he'd fallen from a man who once hadn't thought twice about throwing a full dinner in the garbage because he just wasn't hungry enough, or he didn't like the taste.

That was a different man, though, a different world. That was Viktor Laskov—a person who wasn't the strange, too-thin, exhausted shell that stared back at him in the mirror these days. Viktor Laskov was a man of intelligence, of respect, of worth. How long had it been since he had thought twice about debasing himself just to make ends meet?

The walk to the resort took longer than anticipated thanks to the snow, but he picked up his uniform from the laundry attendant and changed with enough time for coffee and a little oatmeal before his shift. His only reprieve, he knew—not starving to death from the left-over scraps they fed staff. It wouldn't rank a single star for a buffet—but at least it was food.

The meal sat heavy in his gut, and he stared down at the table, peering through small windows of clear vision in his eyes. He rubbed at them, but there was no change, and he supposed it was like being kicked while he was down. He had no hope of being more than this now. No real papers, which would protect him if he put up a fuss about the kitchen staff, no money to see a doctor, no insurance, and no vacation.

Just day in and day out—the same routine. His hands cracked from the harsh soap, and the only fluent English he spoke were the insults thrown at him when the cooks had no one to take their bad moods out on.

He made sure to smile though, always. He made sure not to let them break him. Not all the way.

Vitya got to work shortly after his meal, clocking in a few minutes early so he could get the bar stocked. He had his cart, cursing to himself in quiet Russian when he saw that no one had bothered to replace the burnt-out bulbs in the hallway. He knew the way by heart, but he inevitably crashed into someone or something at least once during his morning stocking, and he was just tired of not being able to do anything about it.

He was lost in his own world when he felt his cart bump something, and the voice hissing out at him was familiar enough it made his heart jump. Chef Garcia—one of the only men who had never made him feel like less than a person. He didn't talk much, and when he did, it was too often only to yell at the people who couldn't keep up with his demands.

But Vitya liked him—at least, as much as he could like a man he had never spent time with. He had caught glimpses of him on days when his eyes weren't so terrible, when Chef was standing under the harsh, bright lights of the kitchen as he surveyed the workspace like it was his kingdom.

He was beautiful. He was lithe, muscular but thin, soft edges to his jaw which Vitya could see under his thick beard. He kept his hair cut closely cropped, and rarely smiled. When he did, though, it was a vision. His cheeks dimpled, his eyes crinkled in the corners, his full lips stretched wide.

Vitya had seen it twice in the last seven years he had worked for the hotel, and he cherished that memory. If he lost his vision totally, he was sure that grin was the one thing he'd never forget.

He couldn't help flinching when Chef yelled at him, or the rush of embarrassment when he clearly misunderstood what Chef was saying. But Chef wasn't cruel about it, even if he sounded exasperated. There was a fondness in his tone which Vitya cherished. He took the chastisement with as much grace as he could muster, and even managed a smile when Chef told him not to get hurt.

It wasn't easy to walk away. Sometimes Vitya wanted to drop to his knees and beg the man to just…he wasn't sure what. Protect him, acknowledge him—maybe even just speak to him, help him feel like a person again. It was easy to lose his humanity in the face of the disdain and disgust from the people around him.

"God, what the fuck took so long?" came a voice to his right as he came around the corner.

Darla. He flinched as her hand whipped past his face to grab the handle on the cart, and she elbowed him out of the way. "Sorry," he told her, but that was it. Because he had clocked in early, and even pausing to talk to Chef hadn't delayed him. She was being cruel for the sake of it, and even dedicating his life to philosophy, he couldn't work out why people like that got such a rush from abuse.

He didn't linger. She sneered behind his back, but it was the one time he thanked the language barrier—and told himself that was why he didn't try harder. He had a long day ahead of him, and with the way his eyes were not cooperating, he knew it was only going to drag on.

Vitya could remember the day his entire life changed, the day he had been shoved on a plane—which had no business carrying passengers of any kind—and took off from the abandoned field with the promise that he would never see his home again. In a way, it was expected. He had chosen to take a stand—even if it was through an anonymous source. He wasn't a fool to think those men—men like him—were never found out. But what kind of man would he be if he sat back and allowed his country to lose social progress. What kind of philosopher sat idly by? He didn't want to be a dead man being remembered as someone who spent his life sitting behind a desk while others suffered. That wasn't who he was.

He remembered it was autumn. He was sitting in his office and squinting at his students' papers and trying to make out the lines, but they were fuzzy and off centered and he knew he should get it checked out. He thought he had time to do it, but that ended up not being the case. It was shortly after that they found out about him, that the police managed to trace those anonymous publications back to him, because when you pissed off people in that kind of power, you were always found out. They showed up, bursting through his office door, shouting all at once over each other. He didn't understand much except that he was being arrested, and he didn't need to ask why. He knew. He knew that he was also probably going to die.

It seemed like a miracle at first that he wasn't put to death. He hadn't even been given a trial—though if he had, it wouldn't have been fair. But maybe it was the fact that he was little more than a professor—a doctor and a philosopher, no one of real importance, but someone people might miss—that he was given the out.

He hadn't been working with anyone, so they offered him a deal—leave his country and never return, or rot in prison. He knew as well as any he'd only last a few days before they were burying a body in the middle of nowhere. Vitya wasn't really that strong, but he was a survivor. He didn't have much family—an aging mother and a younger sister who had a good job and a nice husband. What would they do to his family if he tried to fight them?

So, he chose option A, and that was the beginning of the end.

He arrived on the shores of the United States after what felt like an eternity trapped in the cargo bay of a plane. He was penniless, with just enough papers to get him a job, and just enough money to shelter him for a few weeks before he took something—anything—that would keep him from freezing and starving.

And maybe it was fear that kept his head down, and maybe it was the fact that his work papers were forgeries and technically he couldn't live there—he was a man without country—that he took a menial job and lived in a small apartment with no heat and brown water and just enough blankets to keep him warm during the frigid nights.

It was the resort that hired him after the diner cut his hours down to nothing, and he knew why. His vision was growing steadily worse to the point he couldn't see five feet in front of him. And it was a problem without a solution because he had no money for treatment, no money to get examined. He had no real identity, no healthcare, and no hope.

So, he did what he could. The hotel owners were nice, and they didn't mind that his English wasn't the best—though he retained most of his lessons from when he was at University. But he didn't want to seem too educated, like he belonged somewhere else beyond the dish pit and dark hallways where guests would never see him.

And it was in those quiet moments he missed home. The soft voice of his sister who would have laughed at him to see him as he was now. "Vitya, you're a fool. You can do better—you can be better. Since when did you give up without a fight?"

And he would be ashamed of himself, except that Katerina lived her life like he didn't exist to protect her husband and children, and he didn't blame her. How could he? It was hardest in the winter—when it was cold, when the holidays were upon them. When everyone around them was hustling and bustling to get things done, and to help celebrate—to make things magical like they didn't live in a cold, cruel world that had people eating hundred-dollar meals while others just outside fought every night to keep from freezing to death.

He had no menorah, no gifts—he had no one to write

home to, no one to expect even the slightest hello from. For his sexuality—for his views on the freedom to exist as he was—he was a traitor to his country, and he didn't think anyone would look favorably on that. He fought for himself—for others like him who wanted to be allowed to live, in the most physical sense of it—to stop being afraid to be who they were. People who wanted to love others—who just wanted to be loved in return.

The archaic fear led to hunting them down—led to men like him, professors with influence over the youth—being shoved into cargo planes with three hundred dollars, two changes of clothes, and a stack of ID papers with a false name and made-up story about who he was. He missed home, he missed his comforts—his apartment, his fireplace, his family—but he'd never regret it.

Not for a million years. Not when people heard what he had to say and maybe—just maybe—he would change the minds of the youth who would far outlive him and the men in power who would have to die someday.

Vitya's hands reached out to make sure the plates on the rolling cart were stacked neatly. The servers often didn't pay attention, no matter how many times the other dishwashers and cooks told them that if Vitya was working, they had to take care. He didn't need another incident. Chef wasn't an inherently cruel man, but he was an impatient one. He was unlike anyone Vitya had ever met, and Vitya would be the worst liar if he said he didn't pay close attention every time Chef was in the kitchen.

He was taller than Vitya, but only by a few inches. He was broad, and Vitya could feel the strength in his hands whenever he helped lift cup racks and silverware bins. His voice was ragged and rough—like a man who spent too many years smoking—and he yelled a lot, but he was always—*always*—patient when Vitya needed time to understand the fast English slang that just never made any damn sense.

It was late—the dinner rush had ended, and most of the guests had gone home. Vitya was long past his scheduled shift, but darkness and cold waited for him at home, so he was far from eager to leave. His eyes were still bad that day, the hallways dimly lit and empty, but he could feel his way along and he was learning to recognize the colorful blurs for what they were in place of real sight.

He took a breath, then headed into the hallway, making his way toward the bar with some reluctance, because Darla was the bartender on duty and she was old, and southern, and she hated him. She hated that he was Russian, that his English was poor, that he couldn't see well, and that he never, ever fought back. He couldn't bring himself to look forward to Tuesday nights at all, except for later, after the restaurant had finally closed, when he would finish cleaning the dish pit and, five feet away, Chef would stand at the expo line and finish his requisition forms.

And they wouldn't talk—not really. He'd ask, "Viktor," because Chef only ever called him Viktor, "was everything okay tonight?"

And he'd lie and say, "Yes, was all good, *solynshko*." Because Chef was his little sun, even if he never planned on telling him that. And Chef well…he never asked.

Approaching the corner which turned into the bar, Vitya took a breath and raised his voice, "Corner!" he called out as he'd been taught to do.

He pushed forward and his cart caught the edge of something—someone, it turned out, by the sound of the yelp. His mind stuttered, not sure if he should save person or plate, and in the end did nothing as they both crashed to the ground. He ducked his head when he heard the plates crash, and he felt a jagged edge tear through his trousers.

He cringed, stepping back, not quite sure if he should go left or right and praying that he hadn't injured a guest or a manager because he needed this job. He hated it—mostly—but he would die without it.

"You dumb fuck!" came a shrill voice, and his heart sank. Darla. "You stupid, goddamn idiot. Why the fuck are you even in here right now? Why don't you watch where you're going!"

"He can't," said that soft, raspy voice that made Vitya's heart start to beat a little harder. He swallowed thickly and didn't dare turn around as a presence loomed behind him.

"No offense, boss, but why the hell is this fucktard even here if he can't see shit?" she demanded with a scoff.

There was a hand on him suddenly, gently squeezing the top of his shoulder, and Chef's voice spoke near his ear with a venom Viktor hadn't heard before. "You can go, Darla."

"But…"

"Expect a phone call from management in the morning. I don't tolerate ableism or bigotry in my workplace. And I don't tolerate slurs." The hand on him tightened. "Viktor. Your leg."

"Is…fine. Promise," he tried, but Chef didn't let go.

"You're bleeding," he replied mildly.

Vitya's face heated and his throat went a little tight. Now that the other man mentioned it, he could feel the sting, and the wet dribble of something down the back of his calf. Panic started to set in because he couldn't afford treatment if it was serious, and if anyone looked into his records…

"Can I look at it in my office?" Chef asked.

Vitya nodded, letting Chef spin him. He appreciated it when the other man let him go, when he walked at a pace that was slow enough for Vitya to follow, and how he kept to the brightest parts of the hallway.

It wasn't Vitya's first time in Chef's office. It was an old storage closet that someone had shoved a desk that took up most of the room into. Iron shelving was still there, and it was laden with huge bags of flour. Vitya could see most of it from the bright, eye-burning fluorescent lights, and as much as he hated them, they allowed him to see a little bit like he used to.

Chef pointed to a chair, and Vitya lowered himself down obediently, making a gentle hissing noise as Chef took his leg, but he didn't fight. He'd been through a lot worse during his rough and tumble youth—likely one of the reasons no one ever suspected him of having dangerous preferences, though mostly it was because no one wanted to look for the signs.

"This might need stitches. I can give you a ride to the hospital if you—"

"No," Vitya said, and grabbed at the collar of the other man's chef's whites. "Please, no hospital. Please. Is fine, I...take care of it. No hospital."

In the clear light like this, Vitya could make out all the planes of Chef's face. The curve of his jaw, the sloping nose, the full lips, the dark, curious eyes. He watched as the tip of a pink tongue wet his mouth, and then watched it settle into a frown. "I can bandage it. I used to be a gir—a scout," and he fumbled over a word Vitya couldn't begin to guess, "but it's been a long ass time since I did any real first aid."

"Promise, is fine. No hospital," he repeated, because the fear gripped him by the throat.

Chef stared at him a while, then dropped his leg and stood. For a brief, near hysterical moment, Vitya thought Chef would turn him in, or turn him over to someone who would force his hand. But instead, he turned back around with a small, blue plastic box in his hands. His long legs folded as he sank to the floor, and with careful, thin fingers he pushed the remnants of Vitya's trousers up near his knee.

"You'll need new ones. I'll write a note to laundry so they don't charge you for these, okay?" he said.

Vitya didn't know what to say, so he simply nodded as Chef's nimble fingers worked a wet, stinging swab over the bleeding wound. He wound a bit of gauze around his fingers after, then pressed it hard against his aching skin, and the pressure seemed to relieve some of the sting.

"Can I ask you something?" Chef said after a beat.

Vitya decided to try a smile, and he saw the way Chef's eyes lingered on his face before he spoke again. "Yes. You ask me anything. Whatever you want."

Chef chuckled quietly under his breath. "I don't...I'm not in charge of hiring here or anything, but you...are you...undocumented?"

And oh, he knew this word, in his mother tongue, in English, in French, and in German. He knew that vile, evil word that assigned value to a person's life—that removed humanity from it. His throat tightened and his breath got a little faster, and he knew he was giving himself away.

But before he could completely panic and lose his composure, Chef's hand on his ankle tightened. "I'm not going to say anything. I just wanted to understand about the hospital thing. If it's fear..."

"I don't," he said, and took a breath. "I can't pay. Is expensive, no money. I have worse injury before, I can heal."

Chef looked a little sad at that, but he nodded, then pulled his hand away to inspect the cut, which wasn't bleeding much anymore. He hummed to himself, then applied three tight, tiny little bandages that squeezed the wound closed. They hurt, they were harsh against his skin, but it meant he was safe still.

One more person had his secret, but as much as he knew it was dangerous, he trusted the man kneeling at his feet. "Thank you, Chef," he said very softly.

Chef looked up at him, their gazes locking, and then he breathed out. "Call me Mario. I mean, I'm not on the clock right now and neither are you."

It wasn't strictly true, but he understood the sentiment. "Mario," he tried out, and the other man laughed.

"I like how it sounds in your accent."

Vitya rolled his eyes. "Is not so different from you." He smiled then, and Mario smiled back, and the moment between them dragged on in a way that Vitya never wanted to end. "You call me Viktor."

"That's," Mario started, then appeared to second guess himself. He stood and took a couple pacing steps back—a habit Vitya had seen, whenever the chef was nervous or uncertain. "Isn't that your name?"

He nodded, glad that he could at least be honest about that. "In Russia we have…nickname? Like…Johnny or Mike. But is a little different. Viktor is Vitya. Friendly, you know?"

At that, Mario's face softened and after a beat, he tried it. "Vitya." The accent was all wrong and spoken in the back of his throat—guttural and Germanic, and yet…he loved it. God help him, he loved it.

"Yes. Vitya. My sister? She call me that. And my mother." He wriggled his ankle back and forth, then sighed when he stepped down and felt a dull throb. It wouldn't be impossible to work on, but it wouldn't be comfortable. "I'm sorry. About…" He waved his hand at his eyes. Even with his formal education, he didn't have the words in English to describe the mess his vision was becoming. "Maybe is better I not work…"

"I like the way you work," Mario said, suddenly fierce and angry. "Don't let that bitch…" He went quiet, then shook his head. "She can say whatever she wants about me, but she can't come at you. You're…Vik—Vitya," he amended, still slow and hesitant over the syllables, "you're *good.* And you're kind, and you work so much harder than half the people on my staff. Don't let her shitty opinions make you doubt yourself here, okay? Am I…does that make sense?"

Vitya allowed himself a small laugh, even if the words Mario had given him threatened to overwhelm him with a feeling he couldn't name in any language. "I understand better than I speak."

"Okay." Mario relaxed. He knelt again, inspecting the wound, and when he was satisfied, he pulled out a roll of gauze and began to dress it. "Just keep it clean, and come in here tomorrow around your break and I'll re-dress it."

Vitya wanted to tell Mario not to worry about it—that he was capable of tending his own wounds. That he had two master's degrees and a PhD and was widely published across the globe. That once he owned a large apartment and had two dogs, and patched up his nieces and nephews after ice skating and hockey.

But he didn't. He wasn't ashamed of his loss, but it was hard to admit those wounds were still fresh. And apart from that—and more importantly—Mario was showing him a sort of affection and caring that he hadn't felt in so long. It created a longing, a desire to drag it out as much as possible.

He was forty-six-year-old man who was melting under the touch of a man close to half his age, and it was shameful. But he couldn't bring himself to care. He'd gone on so long without, this little touch quenched a thirst that was killing him.

"Thank you," he said, his voice nearly a whisper.

Mario didn't look up right away, instead gently running his hands over the gauze as if to tell whether or not it was secure. When he finally pulled away. Vitya felt the loss like a keen ache, and he breathed through it.

"Can I give you a ride?" Mario asked.

Yes, everything in Vitya screamed, but he shook his head all the same. It was one thing to accept these small moments, but greed would serve as nothing more than to make the pain worse when ultimately, it was all over. He rose to his feet, testing his balance and his leg. Annoying, but livable. "Thank you for help tonight, Mario. Please, have good night."

With the phrases he'd mastered with some ease, he nodded his head and let himself out. As the doors closed behind him and he stepped into the cold, Vitya forced himself not to look back.

Chapter 3

The sting of the needle would never get less painful. Mario had come to that conclusion five years almost to the day when he first pressed the sharp point of a syringe into his skin and pressed the burning liquid into his body. It did get easier, though. It had taken him a while to give himself his T shot without really forcing his own hand, but the needles were smaller, and his doctor had showed him how to jab himself in the fleshy bit under his bicep, which still burned like the goddamn devil, but didn't linger the way it had in the muscle of his thigh.

Leaning over, Mario spit the cap of the syringe into the trash before shoving the rest into his sharps container, then sat down on the toilet seat and massaged himself gently until he felt the burning ease up. He stared down at his feet—at his rounded toes, and how flat they spread out as he aged and his arches fell—then looked up a bit further at the thick black hair cascading from his knees down.

Most of it was natural—the testosterone making it grow a little longer, and a little thicker. But his genetics were a blessing in disguise—where women in his family were lamenting the tinged dark hair on their upper lips, he was reveling in the ability to have enough to shave it even before he started hormones.

Today wasn't a bad day. He'd woken up in a decent enough mood, was able to stare at himself in his mirror during his morning work-out routine and not feel that crushing sense of wrongness, which was a plus because he had six doubles in a row for holiday prep and he knew it was going to wear him down.

He was glad it wasn't always that bad. He was glad that most days outside of the Christmas Depression—as he liked to call it—he was just himself. And he'd survived all those other holiday seasons, so he knew this one wasn't going to be any worse than years before.

The biggest difference was, he was distracted that morning. Hell, he'd been distracted all night after watching Viktor—*Vitya*—walk out the back door and into the alley. The service entrance had closed, the ringing sound like a foghorn, warning him of imminent danger. His heart was precariously close to a virtual stranger, and every time he tried to pull back, he was drawn in.

Vitya was something else—an enigma he hadn't quite worked out. His English was a little shaky, but it was obvious he understood far more than he wanted people to believe. There was an intelligence in his eyes—something that went beyond hobbyist learning—and Mario felt an almost desperation to know more.

He crossed a line right after Vitya had gone home for the night, using his credentials to get into the employee profiles, and he found Viktor Popov almost instantly. And…it sounded wrong—fake. Like John Johnson or Peter Jones. Like it was a name picked out of a book that was just normal enough, people didn't ask questions.

His profile was sparse—no family, no education, no

previous residence. It was like he suddenly sprang into being, straight out of a Greek myth, and wouldn't *that* be a kick in the ass. But in reality, he knew what it meant. He was there under shady circumstances, and it wasn't that he was working under false pretenses, but it was the why. What had he done? What was so bad that he had to conceal the truth about himself?

"Do you even really give a shit?" he asked himself as he stood to stare at the bags under his eyes in the mirror that sorely needed a polish. He used his thumbnail to scrape off a toothpaste fleck that sat right over his left nipple, then he shoved his hands under the cold water and washed them with the too-clean smelling orange soap.

He cupped lather in his palms, then sloughed off flakes of ink and skin from his chest before patting himself dry and twisting from left to right. Crusty and sickly, the stag looked like something out of a Rob Zombie horror flick, but it wouldn't last. Beneath the bits of shredded skin was the start to a new image. The ink shone in those spots—smooth, a little bright. He knew it would fade with time, but for now, it would stand proud over his chest—the horns covering his scars, cascading up to the beat of his heart where he proved to the world he lived.

The lotion was cold, but it felt a little soothing where he felt cracked and stretched, and he grabbed his phone to set a reminder to show Mat the progress after work.

The clock told him he had exactly sixteen minutes to be out the door so he could make it to work his customary forty minutes early, because rec and inventory waited for no man—especially not him. And it absolutely—in no way at all—was because Viktor had an opening shift to cover breakfast.

He knew Viktor worked doubles on the weekend—a split shift of breakfast and dinners—and if Mario got their early enough, he could sit in his office with a direct view of the pantry and watch as Vitya stacked salad plates, which would all be used, and dirtied, and some of them broken by the end of the night. It was soothing to watch his rhythmic motions, the way he did each thing so carefully, half by touch, half by what he could see.

He imagined going over to see how he was doing—which wasn't out of character. He'd been checking on the man since he started, and he always worried. But it was more than just concern. It was the sweet way Viktor would smile at him, the way he'd say in that low rumble, "Am okay, *solnyshko*." Little sun. It had taken him weeks to work it out, weeks to type it phonetically into Google until he found the answer. It made his heart beat faster, and his mouth go a little dry. No one had ever thought of him that way. He was a dark rain cloud, thundering around the kitchen, and knowing Vitya saw him in a totally different light was heady. It was addicting.

He felt a jolt then, suddenly, when he realized he'd been watching Vitya for so long now—had all of those feelings simmering deep inside him, and he never noticed. Not until now, until he'd knelt at Vitya's feet—had taken his leg in his hand, had comforted him, did his best to heal him.

How much longer would he have ignored what he wanted if that moment hadn't happened?

Mario was startled out of his thoughts by the shrill sound of his ringer, and he picked it up without looking at the caller ID, knowing it would only be work.

"Do you want to explain this email?" It was Joanne, the woman who would be forced to deal with the paperwork clean-up of last night's incident. "You're accusing Darla of a *hate crime*?"

Mario pinched the bridge of his nose as he walked out

of the bathroom and grabbed his t-shirt and chef's pants from the dresser. "I think hate crime is a strong word, but not totally inappropriate. She was a fucking cunt last night. You should have heard what she called him."

"Was it worse than calling her a cunt right now?" Joanne challenged.

Mario pinched the bridge of his nose, squeezing his eyes shut. He was hit with instant regret, but his desire to be protective over Vitya made him stupid and thoughtless. "You know I didn't mean that."

Joanne sighed. "And maybe she didn't, either. Mario, are you seriously going to pursue this over something so ridiculous?"

"It wasn't goddamn ridiculous, Joanne! She deliberately ignored safety protocols and then used slurs when he tried to apologize for something that wasn't even his fault," Mario said, not letting her go on. No one really liked Darla, but she'd been working there for what felt like two hundred years. She looked like the damn crypt keeper and acted like it too.

"Look, I know you're protective of your kitchen staff—Viktor in particular. And I know you want people to accommodate him because of the whole, no glasses thing or whatever," she said, and Mario bristled because he was pretty sure it was more than that. The way Viktor had reacted to the idea of a hospital meant that even if he was going blind, he wasn't going to get checked out. He didn't need readers, he needed treatment. "But we can't bend over backward because one man doesn't want to get his annual eye exam."

Mario rubbed at his temple. "It's not as simple as that, and we both know it. And it doesn't fucking matter if he couldn't see her. He used protocol. He announced his presence before he turned the corner, and I saw her. I saw her look up, then deliberately step into the path of the cart."

"I can't fire her," Joanne said tiredly.

"Then move her. Give her Tuesday morning shifts, I don't care. But I don't want her on shift with Viktor, and I want a formal write-up." When Joanne took a breath, likely to try and argue again, he said, "You know it's not just this incident, Jo. And you know he wasn't the first person she's come after, either. She had plenty to say about me and my gender when I first started. Her insults are bland, but they're deliberate. And I kept my mouth shut because I'm used to it, and really, it doesn't affect my job. But I will not have her going after my staff."

There was a long pause, then Joanne sighed. "She's outside right now waiting for this meeting. These are serious allegations, so if she wants to take this further..."

"I will gladly step in as a witness and former victim of her bigotry," Mario said.

"Fine. I'll handle it. And thanks for this, by the way. Right before fucking Christmas."

She hung up before Mario could respond, and he slammed the phone down on his dresser, a nasty little part of him inside hoping the front shattered so she wouldn't be able to call him for the rest of the day. Joanne was a good boss, most of the time, and an okay person, some of the time. But she had old-school, bigoted ideals, she would always put the hotel and the bottom line first, and the only thing that really mattered was the resort's reputation.

The only reason she didn't give in now was she knew Mario wouldn't let it go without a fight. Maybe he had the first time, when Darla ran her mouth about him, but not now. Not with Viktor. Not ever when it came to Viktor.

Chapter 4

Mario found himself in the foulest mood as he got behind the wheel and pulled out onto the main road. God help his staff that day if everything wasn't up to scratch. They were doing the Chanukah dinner that Sunday for the second night, and Monday was Christmas Eve. Mario had put his foot down the evening before when Joanne once-again tried to tell him that it was a superfluous expense that no one cared about.

"Like five of my guys are Jewish. Are you seriously telling them their holiday doesn't matter?" he demanded.

She had rolled her eyes at him, turning away to fuss with the espresso machine. "It's a minor holiday. It's a waste of money and I'm not going to sign off on it."

"Fine. Then I will walk, Jo. I'm not kidding here."

At that, she'd looked at him. "You're going to regret fucking with me."

Mario had simply shrugged. "Do your worst." Because he would not back down over this. Not now.

So, she'd agreed, and she signed his forms so he could

order everything he needed to get the banquet set up and scheduled. She was pissed about it—retaliatorily pissed—but he didn't care. There wasn't much she could do to him since she was desperate to keep him on. He was the first competent head chef in years, and her worst was probably hiring a bunch of local kids from the high school to fuck up his kitchen for a few weeks before getting fired.

He'd survive.

Mario turned the corner, the wheels slipping a little on the ice, but he steadied the tires just as he saw a dark figure trundling along in the tall drifts of snow. It didn't take much for Mario to recognize Vitya—his gait, the hunched way he held his shoulders, and that damned grey beanie he always carried with him.

He stopped before he was really consciously aware of it, and he rolled down the passenger window. "Vikt—Vitya," he corrected. "Get in the damn car. Are you trying to kill yourself?"

Vitya looked up, squinting through the too-bright, sunny winter day, then he shuffled forward and opened the car door. "Is fine. I walk every day."

Mario rolled his eyes, in no mood for his willingness to expect shit as the norm. "It's like fifteen degrees out here, dude. And people drive like shit. You're going to get killed."

Vitya let out a tiny sigh, but he didn't argue. He didn't do much apart from using his teeth to pull his sopping wet mittens off his hands and hold them over the vent. Mario's insides squirmed, aching, wanting to reach out and do something about it. So, he did—as much as his inner voice was screaming, '*What the fuck do you think you're doing*!'

His hand curled around Vitya's wrist and he pulled it over, curling his warm palm over the icy, stiff fingers.

"These mittens aren't great for snow. They have no protective leather on them, and they're soaked. You know that, right?"

Vitya actually rolled his eyes and snorted. "You know I'm from Russia, right?" he mocked right back. "I knowing snow better than you. So many months, so cold. This..." he waved his free hand toward the window, "is nice summer day."

"Fucking liar," Mario said, but he was grinning. His bad mood lingered, a gentle simmer in the background, and it would come to a boil once he was on the clock and inevitably everything went wrong, but he let himself bask in the softness between them. "How's your leg?"

"Little sore," Vitya said. He dragged his tongue over his lower lip, and Mario almost drifted, unable to stop staring. After a beat, he let Vitya's fingers go, and watched as he returned his hands to the vent. "I wear mittens because I knit them."

Mario startled, his eyes wide, because he could actually picture Vitya curled up in his shitty little apartment with a pair of needles clacking, thick yarn dragging across the floor from a little ball. "Oh, uh. That's...I never learned how to do that."

Vitya shrugged. "My..." His brow dipped like he was searching for a word. "Grandmother. Teach me. Mama say not for boys, but I like it. It keep me..." He frowned again, but when it became obvious he couldn't find the word, he just shrugged.

"I used to run," Mario confessed, and he was surprised because he never shared details of himself before he left home—before he started the process of becoming on the outside who he was on the inside. "I was on the track team at school." The girls' team, and even then, he hated it—

long before he had the words to explain why. He hated standing in the locker room and seeing bodies that mirrored his own on people he didn't belong with. But he had loved running. "It's been a while since I had time to do it, but it used to clear my head like nothing else."

"You can make time. Try again," Vitya said. His eyes—obviously myopic and struggling to focus on Mario's face, still didn't waver. "Is good for you."

Mario snorted. "Yeah, I know. It would probably kill me now. Well, maybe not. I work out a lot, but I suck at cardio these days."

The conversation slowed to a stand-still as they pulled into the employee parking lot. Mario turned off the car, the heat dissipating almost instantly, giving them a taste of the frozen outside.

"Thank you for the ride."

Mario pulled a face. "You should let me pick you up more often. It's fucking ridiculous that you want to walk when it's this cold out."

"I'm fine when..." Vitya started, but Mario reached out again. He meant to grab his arm, maybe his wrist, but instead his hand landed on the crook of his neck, thumb brushing against his exposed skin, stealing Vitya's words.

"Please. It would make me feel better. I know your eyes are fucked, and it's cold, and winter is shit here. I can do this one thing for you."

Vitya's jaw worked, and his lips parted, then closed again. He took a breath through his nose, then nodded. "Okay."

Mario was startled. He'd absolutely and completely expected Vitya to turn him down, so he wasn't quite sure what to do with his sudden acquiescence. "Tonight?"

Vitya looked like he might argue, then he sighed again

and dipped his head down once in a nod. "Tonight. After shift."

Mario released him before he did anything stupid—like lean over and kiss him. He waited until Vitya was out before locking up. They walked in, Vitya a few paces behind him, and he wondered if it was deliberate, but he wasn't cruel enough to call him on it in front of the lingering employees near the smoking bench.

It was just inside that they parted ways. It was a stark reminder of how different their stations were in life—how equality, in so many ways, was a goddamn pipe dream. Vitya was employed there because it was easy to hide people like him. No one really looked at the dishwashers, the housekeepers, the maintenance staff. They were the ones who kept the place running, and the ones who were never seen. The hotel wanted the attractive men and women up front—the ones who looked like they could be the rich assholes one day. They wanted their guests to feel at home, and he knew none of them wanted to face the realities of what went on behind the scenes. They'd crumble without men like Vitya—but they'd never let their staff know it.

And who was he to start some revolution? Even if the thought of Vitya suffering alone— walking to work in freezing temperatures on an injured leg after nearly losing his job thanks to a mouthy bartender—made his stomach twist and bile rise into his throat. He had no place to make a bigger deal out of it, and from Vitya's reaction to something as simple as an ER visit, he knew the other man wouldn't exactly thank Mario for throwing him into the spotlight. It wasn't up to him—but enacting small changes—that was something he could do. At the very least, he'd spend the rest of his days making sure Vitya knew that—at least to him—he was *somebody*.

Taking a breath, Mario swung by HR to pick up mail, then made his way to his office to begin his day. Just like any other. Just like the day before. Only this time, when he looked up and saw Vitya stacking plates, he let himself smile.

Chapter 5

The day dragged on, and Vitya was used to working under uncomfortable circumstances, but the connection between him and Mario was starting to weigh on him. He'd even stopped calling his boss 'Chef' in his head, and he knew that was too close to crossing a line. Mario was kind, and he was flirtatious, and he was sweet—but he was also young, and that was dangerous. Vitya couldn't afford to be the center of anyone's attention, and knowing Darla had been reprimanded on his behalf had left him quaking with fear.

What if she reported him? What if she wanted to retaliate? He needed this job—he had no backup, no safety net. If he was found, he'd be deported, and then what? After rotting in some immigration jail for months, he'd be sent back to a country that had kicked him out for sedition, and there was no telling what they'd do to him or his family if that happened.

There was nowhere for him to go. This was his one chance at surviving while marked as a traitor, and he couldn't blow it.

So, he kept his head down. He did as he was asked, he took triple the amount of care as he shuffled along the hallways, and he did everything in his power not to draw attention to himself. Luckily, with the chaos of the holidays, people were far too focused on Christmas to give much of a shit what a half-blind dishwasher was doing.

And that was good enough for him. He didn't celebrate the holiday himself—his family had been Jewish for as many generations as they could trace back, and they had never really done much during his childhood for anything apart from the high holidays. So, unlike most of the others who were forced to miss their families for work during the hectic season, he didn't carry the lingering bitterness like everyone else.

It was lonely, yes, but loneliness wasn't going to kill him any more than the small wound on his leg that Mario fussed over not more than a day ago.

The memory made his cheeks heat, and he went to elevate his calf during his lunch break in the employee cafeteria. One of the older breakfast cooks was running the grill in there, and Vitya ordered chicken and some sautéed runner beans before taking up his customary seat in the furthest corner of the room. He had a hot tea, and a small jar of honey, and the quiet of the late afternoon when almost everyone was at home resting before the dinner rush.

He hadn't had the freedom or privilege to spend his breaks somewhere softer than the cold, too-bright employee area since he'd started working at the resort, and honestly, his home wasn't much more welcoming as it was. The place had only just been rebuilt from a massive roof leak, which had ruined his walls and destroyed what little he had for himself, and it was by miracle alone he'd been able to air out most of what he had without ruining it.

He'd spent a week going from shelter to shelter, and even spending a couple of nights on a park bench before he'd been allowed to return to his home. Even with nothing, it still felt like something, but it wasn't a place he wanted to spend a lot of time.

Still, many didn't have even that, so he reminded himself to be grateful, even on afternoons like this where all he wanted was a soft place to lay his head. He closed his eyes, sinking into a darkness that he had chosen rather than the blindness pressing him on all sides, and he heard the faint sounds of Christmas music coming from the lobby.

Christmas had never made much sense to him. It was a big holiday back home—the lights in the city, St. Petersburg, aglow with them strung on every building and around every pole. You couldn't turn the corner without knowing it was Christmas, and in a way, it was isolating. There weren't a lot of men like him in the city, and just like now, his traditions were ignored. But he still had fond memories back when he was teaching. His students had always adored the diversity of winter celebrations, and he'd always encouraged them to decorate his office as they saw fit. A few years he'd even brought in Chanukah cookies and told the bloody, terrifying war story that had transformed itself over the years into a miracle of oil and lights.

They loved it, of course. Lapped it up and asked for more, and he felt wanted and appreciated.

What a foreign idea that was to him now.

He laid his arm on the table, resting his temple in the crook of his elbow and let himself drift. If he couldn't sleep, he could at least stay only half awake until he was needed again—and then he would repeat. Likely until the day he died.

He tried not to dwell on it, otherwise he thought he might just crack.

"Vitya?"

It was the voice he both did and didn't want to hear with a desperation that startled even him. Vitya blinked his eyes open, and he could see clear enough in the bright, harsh light of the employee room as Mario loomed over him. Vitya didn't often get the chance to see him that well. The hallways were impossibly dim, and behind the line in the kitchen was even worse.

Now, he drank in the sight. Mario's soft, brown skin, his thick, neatly trimmed beard, his shorn hair just a dark shadow over his round skull. His jaw was sharp, nose tipped up at the end, and his eyes were like a rich coffee—nearly black as they regarded him with some hesitance.

"You needing me?" he asked, trying to lift himself up.

Mario's hand lifted, hesitated, then fell to the back of his neck. In spite of himself, in spite of the fact that he knew he was playing with fire, Vitya relaxed into the touch and didn't pull back when Mario sank into the chair next to him.

"I just wanted to check on you. I was worried."

Vitya couldn't help a small laugh. "You like mama bird, always flying in, flying out. Is small scratch, okay? Leg not falling off."

Mario's lips twitched into a half-grin, and *God*, he was so beautiful. "Stranger things have happened, you know. But I also know you had to be tired after all that last night. You could have called in sick. I would've had your back."

Vitya's nose wrinkled. "Have rent, need to work many hours," he told him simply. It was more complex than that. Since the incident with the roof, his landlord had been an even bigger tyrant—desperate to cover the bills he'd been forced to pay due to his own negligence. Several of the tenants had moved out after the leak, and he was all-but crashing down their doors on the first if everyone left hadn't paid the moment his office door opened.

It was a lot, and Vitya felt like he was on borrowed time with that place.

He didn't miss the look of sympathy in Mario's eyes, either. It wasn't quite pity, but it still stung just the same. "Is there anything I can do?"

"Not send me home," Vitya told him. It was an easy answer. "Need hours."

Mario drew his lower lip between his teeth, then nodded and shrugged. "Okay. I just don't want you to overdo it. You don't usually work Saturdays, right?"

Vitya furrowed his brow in thought. No, normally he didn't work Saturdays—his one concession, even if he didn't exactly keep the Shabbat in every way, he tried his best to honor it. But there was something happening at the hotel, and he couldn't remember if he'd been scheduled. So, he just shrugged at the other man.

"No, is day off."

"I have a Chanukah dinner planned for Sunday and I need help with the banquet prep."

Vitya leaned up on his elbow, a little surprised because the holiday had gone largely unnoticed in the years past. "Why?"

Mario frowned. "Why what?"

"Why Chanukah? No one here celebrate."

At that, Mario actually looked angry, and he pulled back. "Jesus—why…you know what, just because *you* don't celebrate doesn't mean it's not worth at least giving a few hours to. I'm so fucking sick and tired of people…"

"Wait," Vitya said, holding up a hand. "Am…is *my* holiday. But no one celebrating before. So why now?"

"Because I'm an asshole and I should have done better

than this last year. And the year before," Mario told him, but his tone had calmed down and he almost looked contrite. "Sorry, I didn't know you were Jewish."

Vitya merely shrugged, because he *was* that—but he was a lot of things that put a target on his back, so why acknowledge just the one without the others? "Is not important."

"It is," Mario insisted.

Vitya studied him a moment, and right then he reminded Vitya of so many passionate students in the past. Ones that wanted to make a difference, to do something that would solve the problems of the world. And most of them had their spirits broken long before they were finished with their education, and he didn't even need to be the one to tell them that, in the grand scheme of things, nothing would matter. People were and always would be seeking ways to subjugate the ones they found inferior.

Taking a page out of Mario's book, Vitya sat all the way up, then reached out with a slow hand and laid his fingers over Mario's wrist. He felt the other man tense, then relax under a gentle stroke of fingertips across warm skin. "People don't matter," he started, and Mario snorted a laugh, but he didn't stop talking. "If is important to me, is important to me. If they don't like, doesn't change for me. I don't need hotel stranger to tell me if my belief matter."

Mario's eyes dropped to the table, and his wrist gently dislodged from Vitya's hand. But just as Vitya was certain the other man was pulling back, Mario turned his arm, dragging back until their palms lined up and fingers sank together in a delicate lace. "That is probably the smartest thing anyone has said to me in a long time."

Vitya raised a brow, then laughed and shook his head. "I study…philosophy before. Long time ago," he said. He wanted to bite his tongue, to stop his words, because he wasn't supposed to share like that. But Mario seemed so lost right then, so young, and Vitya couldn't quell his desire to guide him. Not like a teacher, but something more intimate. The thought should have terrified him, but seeing the way Mario's eyes softened, the way tension bled out of him, just made him want more.

"What did you do before this?" Mario asked, his voice a quiet murmur.

Vitya's cheeks heated. "This is maybe…not place? To talk about the past."

Mario ran his tongue over his bottom lip, and Vitya tracked the movement before looking down at their joined hands. They fit—Mario's slightly smaller but just as rough, just as calloused from years of working with them. His skin was darker than Vitya's, the contrast more stark in the harsh light of the fluorescent bulbs above them, and he didn't want to look away.

"Some other time, then," Mario said after a beat.

Vitya nodded, saying nothing, and after a short forever, Mario's hand left his with a slow drag of palm against palm. His breath hitched in his chest, and he didn't dare look for up for fear of seeing the same desire mirrored there. With proof that Mario wanted him back, he wasn't sure he had the strength to stop himself from taking that last step over the line.

Chapter 6

It had taken all of Mario's self-control to walk away from Vitya in the employee lounge. But he knew it had to be done. Mostly because he had a mountain of work piling up. They were officially at capacity for their Christmas Eve dinner, and even the Chanukah dinner was gaining a little traction, which he would gladly throw in Joanne's face the next time he saw her. He had a phone meeting with a rabbi soon, and he was hoping the word would spread further after talking to him.

His F&B director had been blessedly absent most of the day, which meant she was likely nursing her wounds after sending an unhappy Darla to the shit shifts, but Mario didn't regret throwing his weight around. He was tired of people treating the job like it was a grandfathered cellphone contract. These assholes weren't tenured—they didn't get to retain old, shitty, nineteen-eighties behavior without consequence. Not in his kitchen, and if his bosses wanted to push the issue, he'd gladly find somewhere else.

Hell, he had a standing offer at the little Greek place up the road since the head chef there was eyeing a job back in London and the owner, Niko, was starting to panic a little. At the very worst, he could commute to Denver every day. He wouldn't be losing much—except Vitya, and as much as he wanted to pretend like that meant nothing, he knew the truth. Vitya had the power to hold him there.

Before, he wouldn't have mourned seeing the backs of any of these people, but now—it felt like leaving Vitya to the wolves. Maybe, though, he could take Vitya with him. A foolish idea—and probably crossing some sort of professional line that would have gotten him incredibly fired and banned from any decent kitchen if Vitya were anyone else but a visually impaired immigrant with shady legal status. He wasn't sure Vitya would complain, though.

But that was a problem for another day.

He eyed the inventory sheet, the schedule, and the prep list and knew it would be an actual holiday miracle if they managed to pull it off. And as it was, the Chanukah menu was looking a little sparse. His own fault, he knew, for not doing actual research into the holiday before insisting on throwing a party. Pastry was whipping up some Israeli doughnuts and some other sweets he couldn't quite pronounce, and he knew latkes would feature on the menu, but he had no idea what the hell else actually meant Chanukah.

"I fucked up," he muttered to himself. Two days gone and nothing more than a load of briskets waiting to be cooked—and what if brisket was offensive? What if it was a meatless holiday? What if…

He heard the trundle of Vitya's cart in the hallway, and Mario shot to his feet, skidding into the hall and looking around wildly. He found the other man twenty feet ahead, marching forward until he came to a stuttering halt when the cart connected with a partition some of the banquet people had moved into his way.

"Sorry," Vitya was babbling. "Sorry, not mean to hit. Are you injured?"

Fuck. He was apologizing to a *wall.* Mario's heart swelled and he felt a strange mixture of secondhand embarrassment and something so endearing, it actually hurt as he rushed over. "Vitya, hey. That's not a person," he said, pitching his voice low in case anyone else was around him.

Vitya turned his head, eyes narrowed as he tried to focus on Mario. "What?"

"That's a...banquet left a partition from that wedding reception last night. It's...you didn't hurt anyone. It's just a piece of portable wall."

Vitya's cheeks lit up like a candle, flickering pink and splotchy. His gaze darted to his feet, and his hand on the cart gripped so tight his knuckles went yellow-white. "Oh."

Mario felt gutted that he'd managed to embarrass him along with everything else that day. "Come to my office later. I'm having a crisis and you might be the only one who can help me."

Vitya looked up, a brow raised, like he was uncertain Mario was telling the truth. "Crisis of philosophy?"

Mario allowed himself a genuine laugh. "More like crisis of food. Chanukah food. I wanted you to take a look at the menu and see where I fucked up."

Vitya looked a little suspicious, but he nodded. "After dinner rush, I come."

I come. It wasn't meant to be heard that way, but Mario couldn't help himself. He was so, absolutely fucked. "I'll be waiting. Have a good dinner shift, man."

Vitya merely nodded, then walked off down the hall, carefully making his way around the inconvenient wall.

Vitya was grateful to not have to work near Mario during the dinner rush—not just because he knew Mario wouldn't go easy on him, as the chef never went easy on anyone—but also because he was still reeling with mortification. Normally, he could tell the difference between people and walls, but the incident with Mario had distracted him and he just recalled feeling something soft collide with his cart.

He was terrified of another incident, terrified of being called out, of being dragged into a meeting, of being outed for his fading vision. What if they demanded he see a doctor or lose his job? He couldn't fake it any more than he was now. And apologizing to a partition was only proof that he was working there on borrowed time.

To make matters worse, Vitya had woken up with a stuffy head and an aching throat, which was the first sign he was coming down sick. His immune system was strong, but winter usually took him down at least once, and it seemed now would be the time. He wanted to pretend like it was nothing, but by dinner shift the chills were setting in and his body was aching.

He muscled through, like he always did, without complaint and as swiftly as he could. He was left in the dish pit for most of the service, which made his job much easier, handling all of the glasses, plates, and silverware easily by touch and not worrying about sending crates crashing into people or onto the ground. But his muscles were screaming at him by the end of the night, and he had nearly forgotten he was supposed to meet with Mario when his shift was over.

When he found the chef's office empty, Vitya trudged to the locker rooms and quickly changed into his sweater and jeans, leaving his soiled uniform with laundry before heading back into the service corridor. Part of him hoped Mario had forgotten—not just because he was feeling bad, but because resisting the other man was getting more and more difficult with each passing hour.

He couldn't stop thinking of the way Mario touched him—a gentle firmness that grounded him in the moment. Mario's fingers had brushed across his skin without hesitation, without disgust or fear, and it was such a new and strange thing to accept.

He was wanted, on some level, by a man who should not want him at all.

He knew the trouble it could cause—for him, for Mario—fraternizing with the boss was strictly off limits, and Vitya couldn't afford the risk. But what he would give for only a moment.

He stopped at Mario's office door, finding it closed, and he pressed his ear to the door and heard the faint sound of music playing. With a breath, he lifted his arm and knocked, dismayed at how much effort that small gesture took, and he leaned against the wall, waiting for Mario to answer.

"Hey, I'm glad you...*shit.* Viktor?" He hadn't called him Viktor since the night he was injured, and he blinked slowly up at the other man who was standing against the light, casting a shadow over his face. "Hey, are you okay?"

Vitya swallowed, grimacing at the pain, and he shook his head. "Just think...am sick."

Mario grabbed his wrist and yanked him into the office, closing the door with a firm click. After a beat, he was dragged into Mario's arms, chest-to-chest, and he felt the other man press lips to his forehead. It took him a second to realize Mario was testing his temperature, not kissing him. "You're burning up. Have you taken anything?"

Vitya swallowed again, shaking his head. "No. Not…I forget."

Mario eased him down to a chair, walking away, and in his hazy vision, Vitya watched him rummage around his desk and finally return to kneel by his hip. "Here," he said, pushing a couple of pills into Vitya's hand. "Take this for the fever, and I'll grab you some tea. I just put my kettle on."

Refusal was on the tip of Vitya's tongue, like it always was, but he was just feeling too poorly to voice it. He dry-swallowed the pills, which went down with ease, then he leaned his head back as he listened to Mario pour water into mugs. "I," he started, but before he could say anything else, a sneezing attack hit him, wracking his entire body. His already feverish muscles seized, and he groaned, unable to stop himself from reacting to the discomfort.

"Jesus, okay that's…have you had your flu shot?" Mario asked, then he laughed behind a sigh. "Fuck, of course you haven't. Are you steady enough to walk to the car?"

Vitya frowned, everything hazy, but he nodded all the same. "I can…I walk home. Is fine."

"Yeah, no," Mario said, grabbing his elbow to help him up. "It's snowing outside. Come on, I'm done here anyway."

It was nice to have a guiding arm, to let his eyes just go soft and blurry, to trust the shoulder under his fingers to get him where he was going without walking him into walls. It was nice to relax and not care, and know for just a little while, someone was looking out for him.

He settled into the comfortable seats of Mario's car, and he let himself drift as he felt the car pull onto the main road. The pace was slow, but the heater was warm, and the medicine was taking the edge off the chills and aches. By the time they pulled up to the curb, he was a little more himself, even if he knew it was temporary.

"Thank you, I," Vitya began as he pushed the door open, but even with his poor sight, he could tell he wasn't home. They were parked in front of one of the townhomes near the older side of the city, with the brick walkways and creeping vines. Vitya liked to stroll there in the spring, watching the flecks of light shine through the tree canopy and play with shapes in the shadows. "Where…?"

"Your place is cold and shitty," Mario said. "No offense. You've probably got the flu, and I don't think I could live with myself if I just let you go home."

Vitya frowned even as Mario came around and took his hand. "I not die last year. Or year before. Am strong, you know."

Mario let out a humorless laugh and tugged him toward the three steps which led up into the building. "Yeah, well, you don't need to be strong right now. Please don't argue. You're going to lie down and I'll make some soup."

Mario reminded Vitya of his sister right then, and it was a vicious wave of homesickness that almost took out his knees. But he managed the steps and appreciated just how well-lit Mario's place was. It was also sparsely furnished, which meant less knocking his shins and tripping over things, not that he'd be doing much getting up.

The fatigue of the long day and the illness was setting in fast, and he didn't fight Mario at all when he eased him down to the sofa cushions and wrapped him in a thick blanket. "Are you allergic to anything?"

Vitya's brow furrowed as he tried to make sense of the words. "N…no," he said, trying to think. "Cat, but I'm love them anyway."

Mario chuckled and he knelt onto the floor beside him,

arranging the throw pillows so he could recline back. "I'm not going to feed you cat. Also, I don't have pets." Vitya's eyes closed as Mario's fingers brushed over his forehead, pressing down as they tested the heat, and then dragging down the side of his face, along his jawline. "Just rest," he said, his voice a quiet murmur. "And call me over if you need anything."

Vitya managed a faint hum before he sank into blackness, and it was with an irrational hope he let himself sleep, hoping he'd wake and never have to leave.

Chapter 7

Mario had taken care of sick people plenty of times during his life. When he was little, his cousins would always be sent over when they had a sick day at school—and it was how he learned to perfect his mom's tortilla soup recipe. A thin broth with only hints of spice, richly seasoned chicken breast, and just a little cheese would be exactly what Mario needed to get Vitya through the first leg of this virus.

He'd done the same for roommates in college, and friends years later who always called him when they felt like shit. But this was the first time in his life Mario had ever brought someone home to care for. It had seemed like such a good idea at the time—like nothing could possibly go wrong., But that feeling didn't last. Not when he couldn't stop himself from brushing his fingers over Vitya's warmth, not when he wanted to slip under the blankets and share skin-to-skin contact to bring his fever down.

It was more than just wanting him healthy, and he couldn't deny it anymore.

Hell, he didn't *want* to.

But he also knew that being Vitya's boss, holding the safety of his job in his hands, put Vitya in a terrifying position. He had no idea how to properly convey that he would never, ever do anything to hurt Vitya at work. That if they tried a relationship, if they took that step and it didn't work, Mario would never want to hurt him.

He was a cruel bastard behind the line of his kitchen, but he cared about the people who worked for him. No matter what.

And Vitya was far from an exception.

Distracting himself with the soup, Mario was frustrated when he came to exactly no conclusions on what to do, except that he needed to feed this man, get him on the path to recovery, and also figure out his work problems. He still had no menu for the Chanukah banquet, and he knew that at least two of his line cooks would call in sick Christmas Eve. He'd have to be a hardass then, he'd have to make those terrible choices and put people's livelihoods at risk, because he had no other options. He'd given as many people the night off as he could, and it gutted him knowing people were missing time with their families to serve these rich travelers who didn't give a shit where the food came from, or who cooked it, or what their lives were like behind the scenes.

Mario felt himself sink a little deeper into despair as he ladled the broth over the tortilla strips, then he added a light sprinkle of cheese before setting it on the tray and carrying it out. Vitya was still asleep, but he stirred as Mario set the bowl down, and his eyes blinked open, staring as if unseeing.

"Where," Vitya started, then recognition crossed his face. "Mario?"

"I made some soup. You've been out for a few minutes." He dared to touch him again, the inside of his wrist pressed to his forehead. Still warm, but cooling at least. "You think you can eat some?"

Vitya nodded, so Mario bundled the bowl in a tea towel, placing it in Vitya's hands, and watched as he carefully tested it. His breath hitched the way it always did when someone new was trying his food—and not just his restaurant menu, but something that was part of him. He could recall hours and hours spent at the stove, making his own broth, adding spices pinches at a time until it was just right. He couldn't erase the look on his mother's face when she realized he had surpassed her cooking.

And at the time, she'd loved it. She thought it was the mark of him getting ready to be like her—a soft-spoken housewife with a few kids, whose greatest accomplishment was taking on Karen at the PTA bake sale and winning.

He'd taken bits and pieces of that life with him. He wouldn't hate being a PTA dad someday—he wouldn't mind blowing Karen out of the water with his Oaxacan chocolate s'mores brownies he'd perfected during his stoner freshman year of college. He loved cooking. He wanted to use his food to help make his house feel like a home someday. Just…not at the expense of who he truly was.

And that was the crux of it, in the end. Not just the fear for what Vitya might have to go through if put in the position to accept or reject his advances—but Vitya rejecting him for his body, and then…and then maybe lying. Out of fear for his position.

His stomach twisted, and he took a few breaths to calm down. When he finally looked up, Vitya had finished almost the entire bowl and had a small, contented smile on his face. "Thank you, was best I ever have."

In spite of his nerves, Mario found a genuine smile as he took the bowl and set it down on the coffee table. He debated about moving, letting Vitya settle in, but the man took the opportunity to snuggle against him, and Mario couldn't bring himself to pull away.

His hand came up without really thinking about it, stroking through Vitya's hair, which was deceptively soft. He let the locks curl around the tips of his fingers and catch on his callouses, and he never wanted to stop.

"Do you miss your home?" he asked after a long silence.

Vitya let out a quiet sigh, then shrugged against Mario's side. "Sometimes. I…have nothing there. I lose everything."

"Why?" Mario asked, keeping his voice low, afraid to break this spell. When Vitya tensed, Mario resumed stroking over his scalp. "I'm not going to judge you, and I'm not going to say anything. I just…I'd like to understand." Because maybe—just maybe—if he could be trusted with Vitya's secrets, he could trust Vitya with his own.

There was another pause, this one longer, and he was sure that was Vitya's answer. Then, the older man turned, pushing his face into the side of Mario's shoulder and breathed him in. "For many years…was not so bad. They encourage men like me. Philosophers. Exploring…" Mario lifted his hand, making a swirling gesture at his temple and drawing it up. "All type of thought—from the past, from the future. Was social reform. But…there was change. Political change."

Mario squeezed his eyes shut, because most of the time his very existence was a political debate. There was no escaping it—so he knew. God, he knew. "Yeah. I get that."

Vitya sighed again. "Someone finding out about me. I'm never have…partner. But they find out I like men through a publication—it was…" He stopped, like he was searching for the word. "Not know who write it?"

"Anonymous?" Mario offered.

Vitya nodded. "I was professor of philosophy. Have three degrees, I study in France, in Germany. Speak many languages. In Russia, I have nice home, nice car, good family. Then they find the paper—someone find me. They say I stir up trouble, that I'm seditionist. They put me in a plane, fly me over the sea. Journey was so long, was so sick. Little food, little water. I'm arrive here at the States with fake papers, little bit of money. So, I run, far from where I land, disappear. I find nice job here, little apartment. Is fine."

But god—*god*—it wasn't fine. It was so far from fine. What was he saying? He committed treason and he was exiled? It was barbaric, but Mario also knew then just how lucky Vitya was to have escaped with his life. "So, your name…?"

Vitya let out a small laugh. "Viktor—they let me keep. Is common name, no one ask questions. The other…" He shrugged. "I take it. It keep my family safe."

Mario almost asked about his wife and kids, then he remembered in the midst of all that, he'd also come out. "You like men?"

Vitya tilted his head back, a faint pink dusting to his cheeks. His eyes were red, and the tip of his nose, and he sniffed before giving Mario a flat look. "I like men, yes. I like you. You not notice?"

Mario couldn't stop his laugh, turning to bury his face in the side of Vitya's hair. "Shit. Yeah, I noticed, I just…" He sobered quickly, because it was everything he wanted, but the definition of men meant so many different things to so many people, and he was terrified of knowing the truth. And he was terrified of not knowing. "There's stuff about me that you don't know yet."

"I'm know you're boss," Vitya challenged.

Mario rolled his eyes, smiling because with Vitya, he felt good. He felt like there was a connection between them, like he could share all the pieces of himself without fear. "I don't know how to—so there's this thing. This word in English. Transgender…"

Vitya scoffed. "Am not child, Mario."

"I wasn't sure you'd know what it means. I mean, English…uh…I know it's hard for you to get certain words."

Vitya pulled all the way back, setting his hands outside the blanket in a prim fold, and fixed his myopic gaze on Mario. "I'm think I know already, but explain to me in your words."

Mario felt a rush of gratitude mingled with surprise that Vitya now knew—he obviously knew—but he was putting the moment solely in Mario's hands. "I'm a transgender man and that means my body takes a little more work to look the way it does. And I'm also gay. I've had some shaky relationships with other men, so I guess…" He let out a tense laugh and rubbed the back of his neck, shrugging. "I guess I'm a little nervous." But less than he had been in the past, he realized. Because it was already so different with Vitya. "I don't always tell people right away, but you shared a lot with me tonight, and I want you to know that all of that—you can trust me with it."

Vitya studied him a long time after he fell quiet, and Mario couldn't be sure if he was trying to see him, or if he was actually looking. Then, he let out a soft sigh. "You nervous is why you're not want me?"

"What? Of course I want you," Mario blurted, a little thrown off. "Shit, Vitya. I *do*. But I've been down this road before, and it sucks to have someone into me, and then it all changes because of my body."

Vitya shifted a little closer, leaning in, letting his hand brush against Mario's, which was warm and sweating from his nerves. "You're man. I like men. I like you," he repeated.

Mario wasn't quite sure he trusted him just yet. Because that wasn't the first time he'd heard those words. But there was a sincerity there that had been distinctly lacking in the other men he'd hooked up with in the past, and he clung to it.

"I," he started, but Vitya turned away, falling into a sneezing fit as he buried his face in a throw pillow. When it was over, the older man let out a miserable moan and flopped his head against the cushion. The moment had passed—for now. Mario detangled himself and hurried to his linen closet, finding a couple tabs of flu medication and a thermometer. It was a little old and over the counter, but it would be enough to help him sleep for a few hours.

And that moment gave Mario a chance to collect himself. He felt hopeful for the first time in so long, he couldn't begin to count the years. A dangerous, precarious place to be, but it was also addictive.

He grabbed water before returning, finding Vitya dozing again, and he knelt down, brushing the hair back from his brow until he woke up. "I have more meds for you, okay? And a thermometer. Mostly you need to sleep. You can take my bed if you'll be more comfortable..."

"Is fine. Here," Vitya said, patting the blanket.

Mario passed over the tablets, then the water, then pushed the thermometer into his ear and saw a mild temp, but maybe not the flu after all. Maybe just a cold—if he was lucky. He'd be up all night though, working on the menu, so he'd be able to keep watch.

"You stay nearby?" Vitya asked when he relaxed into his blanket nest.

Mario nodded. He cupped Vitya's face and ran his thumb under his lower lip. "I'm going to be in my bedroom at my desk working on a couple things. I'm not going anywhere."

Vitya let out a soft hum and nodded. "Okay. Thank you."

Mario cupped his cheek a little more firmly, and Vitya's eyes opened wider. There was understanding in them, and a mirrored want simmering beneath the surface. Mario dipped his head in lower, Vitya raised his own. There was a breath of space between them, a faint pause, and then their lips brushed together. It was barely a kiss—a ghost of a kiss—but there was a promise in it that Mario would die before he broke.

If Vitya wanted him still, once he was better, Mario was willing to give himself over. Mario was willing to let himself have—to let himself take. He'd been alone too many years, and he was ready. If that holiday miracle came in the form of an exiled Russian traitor well... stranger things had happened in his life, and he was looking forward to finding out what the morning would bring.

Chapter 8

Vitya woke pouring sweat and gasping a little, his throat achy and dry, but nowhere near the pain he'd felt earlier when he first arrived at Mario's office.

Mario…

He jolted upright, remembering where he was, and his eyes narrowed in the dark room as he tried to tell the difference between furniture and shadows. He recalled Mario leading him to the sofa, and tucking him in, then feeding him soup and a little medicine. Then there was a hand in his hair as he sank into Mario's arms, and then…

Then there was the kiss.

He reached up with the tips of his fingers, drawing them over his lips like maybe he could feel the evidence there—like maybe they would be able to tell fact from fantasy, because the moment between them had been so surreal. Vitya had told Mario more about himself than he'd told anyone since being unceremoniously dropped on the eastern shores of the United States, and in turn, Mario showed Vitya pieces of him.

Even in the haze of his sickness, Vitya could tell

Mario's confession had been difficult for him. His voice was steady, but there was an undercurrent of fear, and Vitya knew that well. Fear of rejection—even attack if the circumstances had been different. Had they been back in Vitya's homeland, Mario likely would have said nothing for the rest of his life. He would have been living as a very different person.

Clearing his throat, he coughed to loosen up his chest, and was surprised at how much better he felt. It probably wouldn't last, but it wasn't the flu. It was a little virus, and he was over-worked, and under-rested, and his body was reminding him it could only take so much. He felt a warmth pooling in his belly, because although he had ignored himself, Mario had not. Mario had cancelled whatever it was he had been working on for the holiday dinners, and he had taken Vitya home.

He couldn't remember the last time someone had bothered. Not since his childhood.

He missed his mother with a sudden fierceness, but something about being here, in Mario's home, lessened the ache.

Pushing to his feet, Vitya carefully felt around, touching the table, then making his way toward a faint light in the far back of the hallway. He trailed his fingers along the walls, then poked his head in through a half-open door and found a shadow sitting hunched over what he was certain was a desk.

He must have made enough noise, because Mario sat up straight, spinning around to reveal the glow of a laptop behind him. Vitya was too far away to make out his expression, but he heard the soft exhale from Mario's lungs, and he felt his own breath catch when the other man rose—a fluid, graceful movement with lanky limbs and long fingers.

"Hey. You okay?" Mario asked.

He nodded, swiping the back of his hand over his forehead to mop up any remaining sweat. "Think fever is gone."

Mario closed the distance between them, taking Vitya by the shoulders. Like before, he leaned in to press his lips between his brows, then pulled back with a satisfied hum. "Much cooler. How are you feeling?"

"Little bit like," he struggled to find the words in English. "Like train hit me."

Mario laughed. "Yeah, I get that. I skipped my flu shot one year and I swear I was steps away from dying. But you look a lot better. Do you uh…you want me to take you home?"

Everything in Vitya screamed no, screamed for him to stay, and hold a little tighter. "What is the time?"

"Just after one," Mario admitted.

Vitya's brows furrowed down. "You have big day, big banquet to plan. You should sleep."

Mario released one of Vitya's shoulders, the other holding tight, and he dragged a hand down his face. "I know, but I'm so screwed. I have to do this Chanukah dinner and just…I don't know what the fuck I'm doing. I was reading this blog that told me to serve fried cheese sticks and ravioli? That doesn't seem right."

Vitya couldn't help his chuckle. "You wanting my help still?"

"Yes," Mario breathed out. His hand moved to the side of Vitya's neck—an almost absent gesture—and he stroked the skin there with his thumb. "That's what I had wanted to talk to you about tonight. Last night. Whatever."

Vitya opened his mouth to tell Mario he'd be happy to help menu plan, but a yawn gripped him, making his jaw crack with it. He might have gotten over his fever, but his body was desperate for rest, and he wasn't sure how long he could remain on his feet.

"Hey," Mario breathed. He curled his hand around the back of Vitya's neck and gently urged him forward toward... something? The bed, he realized when his shins hit the side of a mattress. He tripped forward a little, his hands falling forward to brace himself, and he sank into the soft foam. "Climb up, okay?"

Vitya turned his head to stare at Mario. "In your bed?"

"I mean," Mario started, and his tone was full of hesitation and embarrassment. "I don't mean...we don't need to do anything, but you need sleep. I can take the couch."

Vitya reached for him, managing to grab his wrist before he could back away, and he tugged. "*Solnyshko*," he murmured when Mario's knees made contact with his own. "Stay."

Mario breathed out. "I looked up that word once. *Solnyshko*?" He butchered the accent, but Vitya couldn't bring himself to care when he was hearing the sound of his mother tongue on the other man's lips.

"Sunshine. My sunshine," he admitted, because why hide it now that Mario admitted he already knew.

Mario went pliant as Vitya scooted across the bed and made room for the other man to follow. It was cold in there —colder than the living room, and Vitya took no small pleasure in burrowing under Mario's soft blankets. His place was far nicer than he'd seen in years, and he had an inexplicable urge to beg Mario to just let him stay there for the rest of his days.

"Comfortable?" Mario asked after he was settled, propped up on his side, looking at Vitya in the dark.

Vitya let out a soft laugh and nestled a little closer. "*Da*."

"Means yes?" Mario asked, his voice a soft murmur in the quiet of the dark room.

"Mm." The exhaustion was climbing over him, adding weight to his bones, allowing him to sink into a comfort he hadn't felt in far too many years. When Mario's hand made its way into Vitya's hair, he rumbled in his chest and pushed into the touch. "What you wanting to ask?"

"Oh." Mario let out a breath, but he didn't stop touching Vitya in some way—pushing his fingers along his scalp, tracing his ear, rubbing down the back of his neck. It lit him up from the inside, even as he drifted closer to sleep. He never wanted it to end. "I mean, I feel lost. I want people to sit down and taste the dinner and think of their childhood, you know? I do the same with the Christmas dinner, and I want to give that to others."

Vitya breathed in deep through his nose, then out, trying to conjure up his childhood holidays. Chanukah hadn't been a huge part of it. His parents hadn't celebrated much. The one that stuck out the most was Rosh Hashanah—the honey and apples, the bowls of pomegranate seeds he and the kids would throw at each other. The savory dinners, the laughter, the sweet feeling of a sort of re-birth, even if he was a little too young to fully understand what it all meant.

But he still had something for Chanukah. One memory, tucked far back into the recesses of his mind. He was twenty-two, his last year at the university before he went on to his higher education. Isaak was a photographer—had come from a little town in Germany to study. His Russian was so poor, and Vitya was obsessed with him. He had kept it to himself, but in early December, Isaak had been helping him on a project and Vitya had felt it—the moment between them. It was dangerous, it was playing with fire—far more than he'd ever been willing to face. But suddenly Isaak's hands were on him, tugging at him, holding him.

They were together through the holiday season, the pair of them holed up in Vitya's little apartment for the eight long nights, cooking their little fried latkes with apple sauce, drinking too much wine, nearly burning holes in the rug with candles.

Vitya could remember it like it was yesterday—the glow of the chanukiah in the window, the blackness of the night sky beyond. He stood there with Isaak, the daring reflection of the taller man holding him from behind, leaning in to kiss his neck, pushing a hard cock against his hole—dry and thick and so forbidden.

Isaak had gone after that, had promised to write, but never did. Vitya hadn't blamed him—hell, he was even grateful that Isaak had been the one to cut ties because Vitya was still young, and still far too terrified to take the risk of ever being found out.

That man—that terrified, lonely, twenty-two-year-old version of himself would have laughed himself stupid if he was told he'd be right here today. A penniless immigrant with nothing to his name but his pride and his past. A sorry excuse for a man, going blind, completely alone, but in the arms of the one person he'd ever been brave enough to reach for.

It almost felt like a better life than he'd once had, and that was a bitter pill to swallow.

"You should sleep," Mario told him, and Vitya realized his thoughts had dragged the silence on for far too long.

"I want to help," he argued.

Mario chuckled, then cupped the side of his face and pressed a kiss to the corner of his mouth. "You are helping. And we'll talk tomorrow. Right now, your body needs rest."

The quiet rumble of his voice was soothing enough,

Vitya let himself go. His eyes ached in the corners, and when he closed them, the darkness carried him off.

Vitya woke feeling better, though a little like he'd run a marathon. The light in the room from the tall window made it look like the gauzy curtains had caught fire, and he took a moment to just watch before rolling out of bed.

For a brief second, he panicked that maybe it was late, and Mario had left him to sleep the day away. But as he ventured into the main room, he smelled coffee and heard the sound of someone humming. Mario's voice was raspy, a little like a lounge singer, and he could have stood there all day listening to it rise and fall with the notes of his song. But the night before set his body alight, made him want more, had given him a courage to reach for it because Mario had showed him— unequivocally—he wanted Vitya right back.

His feet were cold on the bare floor, but he made his way across, narrowly avoiding the sofa and the low coffee table as he turned the corner into the kitchen. It was just as bright with morning sun as Mario stirred something sizzling in a frying pan. It had an earthy smell, like mushrooms, and Vitya walked over to peer down as Mario turned his head to greet him.

"Feeling better?"

Vitya nodded, scrubbing a hand down his face. His throat was a little sore, but he was fairly sure the worst was over. "Coffee?"

Mario chuckled, then reached into the cabinet next to him and pulled out a mug. "Help yourself. It's fresh."

Vitya did, savoring the idea of having freshly brewed

grounds at his disposal hours before work, and he took a long drink of the bitter liquid. The warmth soothed his insides, and he let himself lean against the other man as he slowly woke.

"Thank you," he said when half the cup was gone. "For last night. For things you say, things you do."

Mario turned his head just slightly, nosing along the top of Vitya's hair. "Thank you for staying. I like you, and I hope we're still good."

Vitya looked up and offered him a smile, enjoying the way Mario's face lit up at the sight of it. "Yes, I like you too."

Mario laughed once more, putting down his spatula, and before Vitya could wonder why he'd done it, Mario had him by the hips, backing him against the counter. With a deft swipe of the mug, Mario had the coffee out of the way, and he put his hand on Vitya's cheek, thumb close to the corner of his mouth.

"I want to kiss you. I wanted it last night, but you were so out of it, and I was afraid I'd be taking advantage of you."

Vitya's eyes fluttered shut at the contact, but he shook his head all the same. "No. Want you for so long. Is always okay."

Mario was quiet long enough for Vitya to open his eyes, then he ducked his head low. "So…now is okay?"

"Now is good," Vitya said, almost begging.

Mario didn't make him wait. He tightened his grip, then lowered his mouth, and then they were kissing. Vitya's past kisses could be numbered between both hands—more than he'd fucked, but less than most people experienced by his age. Most of his lovers hadn't wanted this from him. They wanted something fast, and dirty. Even Isaak had avoided kissing him most of the time, even if he'd made Vitya's body sing.

With Mario, it was so different. It was soft, and it was demanding, a little sharp when he bit his lip. And, most importantly, it was full of a freedom he couldn't have elsewhere. He was trapped by circumstance, but allowed to have this, and he wasn't sure where the greater tragedy lay.

It didn't matter then, though. Not with the way Mario held him tight—like he was afraid if he let go, Vitya would disappear. Not in the way he kissed him, like he needed Vitya's mouth to breathe. And not in the way he crowded him back against the counter, or the way he slotted is knee between Vitya's and gently nudged his filling erection with the top of his thigh.

Mario groaned into his mouth, his hand moving to grip at Vitya's hair, and after a long forever of short, nipping pecks, he pulled away. "If I don't stop now, I'm never going to."

"I wouldn't tell you no," Vitya murmured, then realized he'd said it in Russian and blushed when Mario gave him an adorably curious look. He wasn't quite sure how to repeat himself in English, so instead he surged in and kissed him once more—a short, furious thing.

"I need to finish cooking. Are you hungry?" Mario asked. He released Vitya, but the echo of his touch remained, leaving him tingling all over.

"Yes." It wasn't a lie, but it was far more complicated because he was starving—but for more than just food. Unfortunately, Mario's kisses had robbed him of any semblance of conversation in the language he struggled with. He hoped his face conveyed what he wanted to say, but if it did, Mario ignored him in favor of throwing eggs into the pan and giving them a stir.

Vitya took the hint that whatever it was between them

would wait until later—he hoped it wasn't going to be an actual forever—and he took his seat at the little breakfast table in the nook near the window.

Now that it was light out, the sun coming through all the windows in the east, Vitya was able to get a good look around. He hadn't missed much the night before, and the little townhouse was sweetly decorated, though more sparse than he'd expected. Mario was such a bright person—Vitya hadn't been wrong when calling him the sun. He was warm, and he was overwhelming—bright and sometimes angry—but all of that together was life-giving.

The place was too spartan for a man like that, though Vitya had no business complaining. His apartment was barely a home at all, it was an empty place matching him on most days when he felt like a shell of himself. But he was warming up now, feeling full and complete in ways he didn't think possible since setting foot on the shores of a country that didn't want him just as much as his own.

"This place," Vitya said when Mario set a plate in front of him, "you're happy here?"

Mario raised his brows as he sat, sipping his own coffee as he pushed his eggs around the plate with the prongs on his fork. "My house?"

Vitya shrugged. He meant it in a more existential way, but his years of study told him most people liked to use their immediate life as a metaphor for greater things. "Very…empty."

At that, Mario blushed, a sweet sort of pink rising from the peppered hair on his cheeks. "I guess I'm never home, so I never decorate. You know? I come here to sleep and eat. I just never felt the need to put up crap I'm never going to use."

Vitya hummed, but he didn't criticize him as he dug into his breakfast. His mind was going a mile a minute, but in Mario's presence, it was easy to focus on one specific task at hand. "I'm help you with Chanukah."

Mario froze, his fork halfway to his mouth. "Yeah?" he asked. His voice was hesitant, maybe even a little afraid.

"Is easy. Not big holiday," Vitya told him, waving his fork before stabbing it through a mushroom. "People want things..." he searched for the word, "...comfort. Latkes, yes?"

"I can do that," Mario told him.

"Meat. Tasting good, tender." He swallowed his bite, then went in for a few more as he tried to recall what his mother would put on the table during shabbat Chanukah. The table would already be laden with food, long before sunset. He could recall staring at the plate of sufganiyot—the oil soaking into the sugars just waiting to melt on his tongue. There would be a fresh, covered loaf of challah, fruits, steamed vegetables, a cheese tray already cut and ready to eat.

Chanukah hadn't been much, but his parents—at least when he was young and wide-eyed—tried to make the shabbat night a little special for him while the rest of the city celebrated Christmas. He would look across the table when they were lighting the chanukiah—watching the way the flames reflected off his father's dark eyes just before he looked down and the blessing danced from his tongue.

He hadn't realized he was speaking until he heard Mario let out a soft noise, and he bit down on the inside of his cheek as he turned his gaze to his plate. "Is not like Christmas, you know?"

"I know," Mario said gently. "I don't want it to be Jewish Christmas. That's not...I know that's not the point. I want it to stand on its own. I just want people to know—even if only two show up—that they're important enough to not be forgotten."

It gutted him, to think what a good person Mario was and know that he'd been rejected by those who should love him. But maybe he was happier here on his own. Mario hadn't asked yet—and maybe he never would. It was a cruel question, after all.

"I can show you challah recipe tonight," Vitya told him, and Mario smiled. "Is very easy. Maybe this one not feed so many, but will be good to use at work."

Mario chuckled. "I think we can do that." He stood, gathering the plates and taking them to the sink to wash up. Vitya knew he should offer to help, but he also knew Mario would turn him down, so he indulged in the moment of peace as he sat and drank his coffee instead. It was a sweet rebellion, one he wouldn't be punished for. In the end, he was rewarded by a soft kiss as Mario's hand, still covered in bits of soap, touched his cheek.

"I'd like you to take the day off," Mario told him. When Vitya's jaw dropped to argue, Mario pressed a finger to his lips. It smelled like lavender soap and a little like dirt from the mushrooms he'd washed. "I'll make sure you have sick-time to cover it. I want..." Mario bit his lip, and there was a look on his face like maybe he didn't ask for what he wanted most of the time, and Vitya felt an almost visceral need to give it to him—whatever he was going to ask for. "I want you to stay here and wait for me. I have a long day, but I want to know you're comfortable and safe. I'll come home around lunch, okay? I have a break from two to five, and I'll spend it with you."

From experience, Vitya knew Mario never went home on his breaks—not for anything. He always worked through them, always pushed himself. This offer, it meant something.

"Okay," he agreed.

Mario looked surprised there wasn't more of a fight,

and Vitya was startled at himself for not giving one. Except, he found it was easy to give Mario what he was asking for. It was easy to acquiesce and allow himself this. Not just because maybe he deserved a little rest, but also because it made Mario happy.

"Okay?" Mario repeated.

Vitya reached up, curling his hand around the back of Mario's neck, and pulled him in for a last kiss. "Yes," he said against his mouth. "Yes. You ask, and I tell you yes. I will wait."

Chapter 9

Mario was absolutely and utterly useless at work. Maybe it was the unresolved sexual tension from the morning that left him throbbing and wanting through the first part of his morning shift, or that he knew Vitya was back at his place waiting for him.

The very thought of the other man in his home, lying in his bed, touching his things, sent waves of possessiveness through Mario that surprised him. His want only increased as his patience decreased, and he could see the relief in his staff's faces when he announced he was cutting out early and would be back in the morning to plan the Chanukah dinner menu.

It wasn't often Mario let himself have time off, that he let himself acknowledge he had a life outside of the kitchen. But this was also the first time he had anyone waiting for him—at least, anyone that he wanted to come home to.

He was an anxious mess by the time he pulled up to his parking space, and his hands were shaking as he reached for his key, fear gripping him as he wondered if Vitya really had waited for him. Mario had lowered his defenses, had all-but begged him to stay, and Vitya had promised. But Vitya also didn't owe him anything, and he was well aware of that. They'd kissed, more than once, and they'd both made it clear they wanted each other. But Mario had held back from offering anything solid—anything with a future—and Vitya deserved better.

He stepped inside and for a moment, there was nothing but silence. Then, as his stomach sank to his feet, he heard a faint humming from the direction of the kitchen. It took everything in him not to throw his keys across the room and run, and as it was, his feet slid across the wood floors as he turned the corner and pushed through the kitchen door.

Vitya was there, wearing Mario's sleep pants, which hung low on his waist, and a t-shirt that was at least a size and a half too big. He looked rested, adorably rumpled, and there was something so sexy about him, it made his mouth water.

"You come home early?" Vitya asked, turning his head with a smile. His hands were pasty white with flour, and there was a bowl of something that looked like yeast bubbling beside his elbow.

"What are you doing?" he couldn't help but ask.

"Try to make challah recipe for you—show you finish bread before we make together," Vitya said.

Mario groaned, walking up behind him, and gave in to his urge to wrap his arms around Vitya's middle and pull him close. "I know how to make bread, Viktor," he said, deliberately using his full name. He nosed behind his ear, then nipped at it.

"Is special," Vitya said, his voice breathy. "Special… family recipe."

"Is that so?" Mario's hand moved from just above

Vitya's naval, to the hem of the pants, then slipped two fingers just inside. He let them scrape along the coarse hair there, thick and long as it wrapped around the tips of his fingers. "You want to show me then?"

"Maybe," Vitya groaned, and Mario felt himself throb again, felt his dick swell, wanting Vitya's mouth on it, his fingers around it. He thought about what it might feel like to hold Vitya down, to slide inside of him, to listen to the way he would groan, make those punched out little noises as he fucked him. "Maybe we…do this?"

Mario closed his eyes, pressing his face to the back of Vitya's neck, and he breathed in deep. "I want to fuck you. Can I…is that okay?"

"Yes," Vitya said, pushing his ass back against Mario's groin. "Yes, I'm want…feel you. All of you."

Mario's shaking hands turned Vitya, crowding him up against the counter, and he kissed him slow and deep, his tongue thrusting in and out like a promise of what was to come. "Wait here. Take off your pants, but otherwise don't fucking move. Yes?"

"Yes," Vitya breathed out.

Mario dragged himself a step back, his hands aching to touch, but he forced himself to look instead—to drink in the sight of Vitya pink in the cheeks, panting, head bowed, and fingers curled into fists. If this was going to be short-lived, if he couldn't have this forever, he would make every single second count.

It took all of his willpower to turn and walk away, but he did it. He rushed into the bedroom, dropping to his knees in front of his closet so hard, he was certain they would bruise. But he didn't mind the pain. It distracted him a little from his throbbing desire as he threw aside old shoe boxes and luggage until he pulled out his small case that had what he needed. His '*fucking dick*'—a name coined by an old friend when he was first trying to figure out how to make sense of his gender and having sex.

It had taken him a long time to figure it out. Experimenting on himself, experimenting with others, learning to trust himself and trust what he wanted vs what he had been taught he should want.

He liked fucking—it felt good, he liked to come. He liked to top—and there were enough toys on the market now that he didn't feel like he was losing out. Like the one he pulled out of the box. It sat snugly against him, a vibrator rubbing his dick while the silicone cock would push deep inside Vitya and take him the way Mario wanted to.

These things made him feel powerful, made him feel like himself, even through doubt and hesitation.

His chef's whites dropped to the floor in a small pool, and he stepped out of them, kicking his boxers to the side as he strapped everything around his waist. The belt bit into his skin in the best way—a reminder of what was to come. His fingers trembled a little and fumbled, but he forced himself to remember that the faster he got ready, the faster he could be inside the man waiting for him in the kitchen.

The man who had obeyed every command.

It was heady.

It was *beyond* erotic.

He swallowed thickly, took a single breath for himself, then put on a t-shirt and a pair of boxers to hide the belt, and grabbed a condom and lube on his way out. His bare feet tapped against the polished floor, leaving small prints behind him, and he made it back to the kitchen where Vitya waited.

Where Vitya waited *naked*, stripped down to nothing. His skin was soft, hairy, olive toned, and begging to have

Mario's mouth absolutely everywhere. Mario felt his dick throb again, and he wished he'd taken time to stroke himself—or let Vitya do it for him—before getting dressed. But he knew, deep down, he wasn't quite ready to reveal all of himself. Probably tonight—or at least soon—but for now, this would need to be enough.

He watched as Vitya's eyes got a little better focused when Mario stepped closer, watched as they traveled down his thin t-shirt, down to the front of his boxers, which were tented with the thick cock. It bounced as he moved, and Vitya swallowed audibly.

"Still good?" Mario asked.

Vitya nodded, blinking rapidly for a second, then cleared his throat. "Yes." His hands reached for Mario as soon as he was close enough, and they first touched his arms, then dragged down toward the slit in his boxers. "You having...?"

After a second, he realized what Vitya was asking, and he drew the cock out. "I want you," he whispered, breathy and a little desperate. His body burned with need to turn Vitya around, to press him to the counter and take him.

Vitya looked down, then boldly touched, curling his hand around it, stroking it. When he looked back up again, there was hunger in his eyes. "I'm...not do this a lot. Before. We go little bit slow?"

Mario cupped Vitya's cheek with a tenderness that surprised him. "Yes. God, of course. We'll go as slow as you want, okay? I want you to feel good."

"And if you," Mario said, stroking the cock again, making the vibrator press harder on his dick, "if this inside me, it feel good for you?"

"Yes," Mario told him, and he was grateful Vitya didn't want an explanation, just a promise that they would both get what they needed.

"How you wanting me?" Vitya said.

Mario chuckled, then pressed a thigh between Vitya's, knocking them apart before raising his to press against his balls. "I'm going to fuck you right here against the counter. I'm going to suck your dick, but you're not going to come. When you're begging me for it, I'm going to flip you around, and I'm going to finger your ass until it's slick and ready, and then I'm going to fuck you."

Vitya's moan was long, drawn out, desperate, and he clawed at Mario's shirt like he was trying to pull it off. Mario felt a beat of panic, and he curled his hand around Vitya's wrist, staying him. "I want to feel, to touch," Vitya begged.

"I...not yet?" Mario asked. "Just not yet."

Vitya sobered, then nodded and went onto his toes like he was trying to simultaneously escape Mario's pressing knee, and sink into his body. "Kiss me."

Mario did. Without hesitation, without a second thought, he pulled Vitya into a kiss with one hand at the back of his neck, the other reaching for his cock, which was hot and so hard against his palm. "God. I can feel how much you want me."

"Will be fast. You touch me...will be so fast," Vitya murmured against Mario's lips.

Mario smiled, then pulled back slowly, sinking to his knees as Vitya released his hold. He didn't have to lean up far to reach the other man's dick, and he let the head smear precome over his lips, chasing the taste with the tip of his tongue before he parted them and took Vitya inside. He could tell already that his lover was close, that there wouldn't be time yet to draw this out, and that was okay.

He just wanted to know him like this, to let Vitya inside a part of him before he claimed him. He tasted like hints of Mario's soap, like the water from the tap, like musk from his sweat, and the faint hint of salt from his slit. When Mario put his mouth around the head of Vitya's cock and sucked, Vitya's hand tightened painfully against the back of Mario's neck.

"Please," Vitya hissed out. "I need...I need..."

Mario rose then, now desperate to be inside his lover. He was close to his first orgasm, and he reached into his boxers to increase the pressure of the vibrator before grabbing the lube and spreading some on his fingers. Vitya let Mario turn him, pressed his hands to the counter, and he spread his legs and pushed his hips back to give Mario access to his hole.

He was hairy—cleaned from the shower, but it would be messy and a little ugly, and rough. And it would be exactly perfect. His finger sank in without much resistance, but Vitya was tense with nerves and even as Mario coaxed him to relax, he shook.

"I've got you. I'm going to take such good care of you." The words fell from Mario's lips, unbidden, vows he would die before breaking. "It's going to feel so good, I swear. I've never wanted anyone this much before in my life."

Vitya let out a little sob as Mario used a second finger, adding more lube, pushing in deeper. His fingers grazed his prostate once, twice, and the noises Vitya made sent him over the edge. His fingers flexed inside of Vitya's hole as his dick spasmed against the vibrator, and he buried his face in the back of Vitya's neck as he stuttered through his orgasm.

"You finish?" Vitya asked.

Mario nodded. "It's fine though, babe. I've got more where that came from. I'm not stopping until you're screaming my name."

Vitya answered with a groan, with a fuck backward

onto Mario's hand. When Mario's palm slapped against Vitya's ass cheeks, Mario added a third finger, then used his free hand to reach for the condom. He tore it with his teeth, expertly rolling it on with a practiced hand, then gently pulled his fingers out.

Vitya groaned from the loss, his head turned to the side and his eyes squeezed shut, and Mario took a moment to just look at him, to appreciate his uninhibited beauty. Bracing himself on the small of Vitya's back, Mario lifted his cock and pressed the head gently against the waiting hole.

"Are you ready for me?"

Vitya nodded, clearly incapable of words, but his body told Mario everything. He wanted it—he needed it—every bit as Mario did.

Mario took a breath, braced himself, then gently pushed. It took a moment for his head to breach the tight ring of muscle, and when it did, Vitya dropped his forehead to the counter and let out a chest-deep groan.

"Okay?" Mario asked, panting. His second orgasm was ramping up, his dick sensitive now, but wanting more, wanting to feel Mario's hips slamming against Vitya's ass.

Vitya nodded, still not capable of speech, but he thrust backward, the motion taking Mario in deeper. His fingers scrambled at the counter, his breathing coming in punched out little sobs. Mario grabbed him by the hips, steadying him, lifting him until he could get his arms around Vitya's chest.

"Do you trust me, babe? Do you trust me to take care of you? To make it good? Because I'm going to make it so, so good."

Vitya moaned and leaned back into Mario's arms, taking the cock even deeper. "I'm…trust. But so much. So…so much."

"I know. But you're fucking perfect, okay? You're taking it so well, you're so...you're so good." His own words overwhelmed him a little by how much he meant them, by how much affection he felt for this man. He clutched at him as he gave short thrusts, feeling the cock sink deeper, feeling Vitya relax bit by bit, taking more and more until finally—*finally*—he was pressed against him.

Mario took a second to breathe, his hands roaming up and down Vitya's chest, gently tugging at his nipples, then scraping his fingers down through his chest hair.

"More," Vitya begged after a short forever. "Please."

Mario didn't need him to beg. He wanted to give this to him more than anything. His hand went lower, curling around Vitya's dick where his erection had flagged a little, but plumped up the moment Mario began to stroke it. He fucked him with short, brutal thrusts, sending Vitya crashing forward against the counter, and his orgasm hit again when Vitya thrust his hips back just as hard.

The cabinets rattled, Vitya's knees hitting the bottom doors, and his cock twitched. "I," Vitya said.

It was the only warning Mario got before Vitya spilled, his head falling to the top of the counter, his entire body going stiff as he came over Mario's knuckles.

Mario realized his ears were ringing only after the sound of the quiet kitchen started coming back to him. The silence was gently interrupted by Vitya's rapid, anguished breaths, and the steady beat of Mario's own heart in his ears. He uncurled his hand from Vitya's softening dick, and he pulled out, though Mario was careful not to stop holding him.

The click of the belt releasing was almost deafening, but there was some relief for his own, over-worked dick as that one fell to the floor. He was sopping wet between his legs, and he was aching in the best way, and the only thing he wanted right then was his bed beneath them, and Vitya pressed against his side.

"Can we take this to the bedroom?" he asked softly, even his whisper too loud.

Vitya only took a second to answer. "Yes. You help... my eyes not good."

Mario didn't need to be asked twice as he carefully led Vitya through the living room, onto the cool sheets that were still rumpled from the night before. Winter was raging, but his body was still heated, so he kicked the comforter to the edge and pulled the sheets up around their waists as Vitya curled into him.

He laid there stiffly for a moment, then gently pushed his hand into Vitya's hair, closing his eyes as he felt his soft waves against his palm. "Was that okay?"

There was silence, then a breathy laugh before Vitya pressed a kiss against his exposed bicep. "Was okay? Was *best*," Vitya told him, his voice a little hoarse. "Was good for you?"

Mario turned on his side, tipping Vitya's chin up with the tip of his finger. The room was dark enough he knew Vitya couldn't see him, but he watched the way the light from the window reflected off his dark irises and realized right then, Viktor was the most beautiful man he had ever seen in his life. "That was the best sex I've ever had." It was an honest answer. He'd come harder, he'd been more turned on in his life—especially when he was younger and his hook-ups were on the verge of hysterical and desperate. But none of them had ever left him feeling like this. Like he'd found a piece of himself he'd been missing all this time.

"Thank you," Vitya murmured.

Mario touched the corner of his mouth with this thumb, then kissed him softly. It was chaste, but lingering, the flavor of them mingled together with a musky sweetness. "Let's sleep for a bit, yeah?"

"Then more sex?" Vitya asked, his hand curling around to touch Mario's ass.

Mario laughed, rolling his eyes, but he knew right then he'd never be able to deny Vitya anything.

Chapter 10

Vitya had gone to sleep in the warm circle of Mario's arms, so when he woke in the bed alone, nestled deep in the thick comforter, it threw him for a moment. Panic set in, like maybe the sex had been terrible, like maybe he'd done something totally wrong and Mario had fled.

It had been new—though Vitya's sexual experiences were few and far between. His holiday lover had been the longest string of steady sex he'd ever had, and that had been years before. With passing laws and growing public sentiment hating people like him, he'd been reduced to closet blow jobs and quick ruts in dark apartments before one of them fled in the middle of the night.

All the same, nothing had ever been like making love to Mario. It wasn't just the differences because his body wasn't like Vitya's, but also there was feeling there Vitya had never experienced, and he didn't even know how to name it. More than once, he'd been far too close to confessing his love, to screaming his adoration for this man. It would have come out in his own tongue, and although

Mario might not have understood, he likely would have been able to figure it out from Vitya's tone.

Because it was true. It was a painful, terrifying truth. He was falling in love with a man he barely knew, and that was the last thing he ever intended. When he left his home country for committing such a grievous sin as to love other men, he had resolved to die alone. Then, Mario had come in, with his fierce glower and sharp tongue and impossibly tender hands and changed all of that—whether Vitya wanted it or not.

He was in this now, there was no turning back.

Pushing the blankets away from him, he stood up and felt along the walls until he found a light switch. It wasn't much, but it was enough so he could find Mario's dresser, once-more stealing clothes that hung loose on him and smelled overwhelmingly of Mario. It had comforted him for most of the day he'd spent alone, but now it worried him.

There was the answer beyond the bedroom door—the acceptance or rejection.

He wasn't sure he was brave enough to face it, but he knew he wanted Mario enough to fight for it.

Stepping into the hall, he closed his eyes and listened, finally hearing movement in the kitchen. He found his way, blinking against the bright lights, trying to adjust as he managed to focus on Mario, who was at his kitchen table. He was bent over, something in his hands, cursing at whatever it was giving him trouble.

"I can help?" Vitya offered.

Mario turned his head, letting out the smallest startled noise, then he set whatever he was holding down and reached for him. Vitya came easily, willingly, feeling relief hit him like a punch to the gut as Mario gathered him into his arms and pressed a kiss to his temple.

"Did I wake you up?"

Vitya shook his head, turning his face up properly for a real kiss. He lost himself in the warmth of Mario's mouth, in the soft heat of his tongue that dragged along his own. He stiffened again, half-hard with a simmering want that he didn't feel pressured to do anything about right then. "I wake up, was alone."

Mario's face dropped. "God, sorry. I didn't want to disturb you, but I wanted to see if I could get this damn challah recipe going before tomorrow. I have to finalize the menu and get the kitchen working on prep, but I just...I can't fucking get this right."

Mario loosened his grip and Vitya peered around him to find challah dough separated into thick strands ready to be plaited.

"It's the braid. It keeps stretching, and one end is longer than the other, and it won't tuck right, and..."

Vitya laughed softly, then carefully maneuvered Mario in front of him, reaching down to guide his hands in the familiar twist and tuck of something he'd done since he was a very small boy. He didn't need to see it—he could plait challah in the pitch-black darkness of some underground cave if he had to.

It made him think of his mother—of the patient way she'd always helped him, and he found himself echoing her words in his native tongue as he guided Mario through. "Just let the bread speak to you, let it tell you where to fold and where to tuck it in. When you stop trying, it will happen."

Mario hummed softly as Vitya's hands guided him, and then he let out a surprised laugh. "Holy shit, I have no idea what you said, but that worked."

Vitya stepped aside, letting his hands touch where his eyes couldn't see clearly, and yes. Yes, it was perfect. Just like the man pressed against him. "Now you rise. Then you bake. See, is simple."

Mario covered the challah, slipping it into the proving drawer, and he was back pressed against Vitya before the other man had a chance to catch his breath. Mario's hands gripped him by the hips, his head dipping low to nose along his jaw, and he let out a contented hum as he nibbled just below his ear. "You're amazing."

Vitya flushed, so unused to compliments like that, he wasn't quite sure how to accept them. But it would feel like the greatest disservice to tell Mario that he felt far from amazing. That he felt so utterly unworthy to be in Mario's arms right then. He was trying to tell himself he deserved this, that he'd earned it after so long of being degraded and hidden and hated, but it wasn't that easy.

"You're thinking too hard," Mario whispered against his temple, then tipped his chin up with one finger and kissed him long and slow. "Can I distract you? We have about an hour before baking."

Vitya wasn't about to tell him no. Something deep inside him still worried this was all on borrowed time, that this was too good to be true and he was never meant for forever, so it took absolutely no hesitation at all to tell him, "Yes. Yes..."

Mario guided him backward, through the kitchen door, to the sofa, which was much closer than the bed. As he touched Vitya, as his hands drew pleasure from parts of his body that he didn't know could feel so good, he started to feel braver, more wanton. He stopped trying to stifle his moans, stopped trying to hold himself back. He let himself touch Mario with pressing fingers against the sparse places of his exposed skin.

"Can I touch...please?" Vitya asked, his fingers toying with the hem of Mario's shirt.

The living room was dark, but Mario was close enough Vitya could make out the war on his face, the struggle. Then, after a beat, Mario took him by the wrist and carefully slipped Vitya's hand under his shirt. "I don't...I'm not ready to take it off, but you can touch me."

Vitya knew what a rare moment this was, what a gift, and he planned to give it all the reverence it deserved. He closed his eyes, and his second hand joined the first, his palms spread flat over the wide expanse of Mario's stomach. His hair was coarse against his palm, short and prickly like it had recently been shaved, and he dragged his fingers over it until he heard Mario let out a quiet, huffing laugh.

"Ticklish," he muttered.

Vitya smiled, then licked his lips and started to trail his fingers upward. Mario's entire body went stiff then, his stomach tucked in, his shoulders pulled back like a reflex. Vitya froze with one palm pressed to Mario's sternum, the second on his ribs. "You want me to stop?"

He heard the click of Mario's throat when he swallowed thickly, then felt Mario sit up a little so he was straddling Vitya's thighs. Just when Vitya thought this might be over, Mario took both of his wrists and carefully guided his hands to his chest.

Vitya wasn't sure what to expect entirely, and he knew right away that Mario's skin didn't feel like his own. He was toned, his pecs rigid with muscle, but there were long bits of dry skin, dipping in places and puckered in others. There was a thin line—he could trace it with the tip of his pinky—and it stretched in a half moon under each nipple.

"Scars," Mario told him after Vitya's hands moved to cup his ribs. "I...those ones are surgery scars. From my top surgery."

Vitya didn't understand all the words, but he knew what Mario was trying to tell him. They were evidence of what he'd gone through to make his body feel like his own. It was gorgeous, and he wanted to tell him so, but the moment was too fragile for that right then.

He simply laid quiet, never pulling away, waiting for Mario to decide where they went next.

"They're totally healed now, so you can touch them. And sometimes I really don't mind who sees them, but sometimes it's a lot. During the holidays I'm already stressed and I just…"

Vitya reached for his face, quieting him with a palm to the cheek. "Is okay. Is fine. Whatever you give me, I want. Kiss me, *solnyshko*. Kiss me."

Mario let out a soft breath, then closed the distance between them, locking his mouth on Vitya's. This kiss was a little more desperate than the one before it, more teeth, more tongue, like Mario was trying to consume pieces of him. Vitya didn't mind, he'd give Mario anything he asked for, without regret and without expectation.

Mario grappled at Vitya's shirt, pulling it up, ripping his mouth away only to latch on to a nipple and bite until Vitya cried out. He was hard against Mario's thigh, a little desperate for friction, but he didn't want that just yet. He wanted to give, not take.

It took some maneuvering, but he managed to get Mario onto his back, one knee between his spread thighs, and he held his face. "I want taste you, suck you. Suck your cock," he said.

Mario shuddered beneath him. "It…are you sure?"

Vitya knew what he was asking, so he dragged his free hand along the inside of Mario's clothed thigh until he was cupping him through his sweats. "I know. I want. Please." His words were perfunctory, not as elegant he could have been in any of his other languages, but it was enough.

Mario guided Vitya's hand to the waistband of his

pants, then let go, leaving Vitya to finish the rest. His fingers curled into the fabric, a slow, gentle tug drawing them down his hips to pool at his calves. Mario lifted his legs when Vitya squeezed his ankles, then let them drop down, his knees falling apart, exposing himself to Vitya.

He wished the light was brighter there—wished he could see him with more than just a touch, but it was enough. He dragged light fingers up Mario's legs, pausing at the junction of his thighs, pressing his thumbs into the tendons.

Mario was hairy there like everywhere else, the coarse strands curling as Vitya's fingers explored further. He was swollen, the scent musky, and as Vitya dragged his thumb between Mario's folds, he felt the way his cock sat nestled there, large and throbbing.

"Want taste you, suck you," Vitya said again, his voice breathy with need. His own cock pulsed between his legs, but he left it there. This wasn't about him right now, and more than he needed to be touched, he needed to get his mouth around his lover.

"Do it. God," Mario begged. Vitya felt him shift his hips, pushing down into Vitya's hands when they cupped his ass and lifted him a little closer. "I need you, please, *please…*"

Vitya didn't want him to beg—at least, not this time. He wanted to hear him cry Vitya's name, wanted to hear him sobbing with need, groaning with release, and he knew how to do that. He dipped his head lower, nosing first along his slit, then opened his mouth and laved his tongue across the needy cock. Flavor burst on his tongue, a soft musk that was the core of Mario. It flooded his senses, and his mouth opened wider, sucking the dick into his mouth. It sat short and fat against his tongue, a perfect fit, feeling like everything he hadn't known he wanted.

Mario writhed beneath him, hands scrambling for Vitya's hair, his gentle tugs guiding him as he punched out little words like, "Yes, just like that, suck harder, more."

When his hand crept up Mario's thigh, his legs parted even further and he shifted, telling Vitya with his body exactly what he wanted. Two fingers teased his hole, gathering up wetness before drifting down between his ass cheeks. He pressed against him there—not slipping in, just circling, drinking in the way Mario all-but sobbed his pleasure. He sucked a little harder, laved the cock with his tongue, felt the way he quivered and shook.

He would come soon, Vitya could feel it, but he wanted to draw it out and make it last. Even if it crashed and burned, he wanted Mario to have this moment—this memory of trembling with pleasure as he tumbled over the edge. He hadn't ever been confident in his skill, but touching Mario's body felt like handling an instrument he was always meant to play.

He knew exactly where to stroke to make him sing, to make him whine, to make him cry.

"Put your fingers in me, fuck me with your hand," Mario commanded.

Vitya wasted no time following the order. His fingers slid in with some ease, only to the first knuckle where he spread them and let them rub against Mario's inner walls. Vitya could feel him start to spasm, feel a rush of warm fluid dripping down the top of his hand as he twisted them, and fucked him. Mario's dick throbbed against his tongue, and then his entire body went rigid, the hands in his hair tightening painfully.

And then he was coming. He pushed Vitya's face against him, his insides clamping down on Vitya's fingers, drawing them in deep as he spilled. It felt like an eternity before he relaxed, his come down impossibly slow, but soon enough he had eased his grip and his breathing hitched in his chest.

Vitya didn't move, only releasing the cock gently and moving his head down to press a kiss to the inside of Mario's thigh. His fingers remained inside as the spasms slowly died down, and only then did he pull out, hearing the way it made Mario groan, and clench like he was trying to draw Vitya back in.

"Okay?" Vitya asked after a long while.

Mario's laugh was ragged and hoarse, but not unhappy. His hands carded through Vitya's hair, a gentle scrape over his scalp, then he tugged until Vitya moved, covering Mario's body with his own. A hand touched his face then, Mario's thumb swiping at his lips to clear up the mess that was left behind.

Then, after a beat, Mario kissed him. He coaxed Vitya's lips open with a careful tongue, dragging it inside like he was gathering up the taste of himself. When he pulled back, he let out a contented hum and pressed their foreheads together.

"That was amazing," he said, kissing the corner of Vitya's mouth. "You're amazing."

Vitya felt his cheeks flush, and he buried his face in the crook of Mario's neck. "Was okay."

"Yeah, I don't have the strength to argue with you right now, so I'm just going to let that one go. But it was so much more than okay." He stroked down the center of Vitya's back like he was the one who needed to come down, and Vitya knew he could get lost in that touch for days if he let himself. "Do you want me to take care of you?"

Vitya shook his head against Mario's shoulder. "Wanting to do that for you. Just you. For now. Maybe later?"

Mario laughed again and shifted so he could tuck Vitya

against his side. He breathed out slow and deep, then touched the corner of Vitya's jaw with the tips of his fingers. "No one has ever made me feel that good during sex before. You'd better be careful, I might not be willing to give you up so easily."

"Don't give," Vitya said. His words came out slurred with fatigue, his body still aching with his recovery, and it was hard stay awake. "Keep."

"Okay," Mario said, but his voice sounded far off as Vitya drifted further. "Go back to sleep for now. I'll keep an eye on the challah, and we can talk more in the morning."

Vitya hummed softly, and a small part of him wanted to stay awake, to draw this out and take more, but he didn't have the strength. He was weak in Mario's arms, but he realized, just before he succumbed, he felt safe enough to let go.

Chapter 11

They fucked twice more before the morning shift at the hotel. *Made love*, Mario's brain corrected as he poured over his requisition emails that morning, and he was grateful for the privacy of his office so no one could see the fuck-stupid look on his face. His body still sung from where Vitya had touched him, where he'd sucked his cock and made him come and dragged out every second of pleasure it until he felt like he might never stop coming.

It hadn't taken him long to revise his previous sentiment that he'd had better lovers. The first time had been with a hesitance in both men who weren't sure what to expect, but when Vitya had pinned him to the sofa and sucked his dick until he nearly cried, Mario knew he was in it.

And it wasn't just the sex. Part of him was too afraid to acknowledge the actual feelings simmering behind the want, but they were impossible to ignore. Vitya was sweet—he was attentive and caring, he was a bundle of nerves almost all the time, and Mario wanted to just hold him and soothe them until he found his calm. He was also intelligent—something Mario realized most people had overlooked because his English was still broken. And it only took a minute to realize why.

Vitya had been ignored—and when people weren't ignoring him, they were mocking him and laughing. No one took time to sit with him, to talk to him. He'd been on his own in his shitty little apartment day after day in the country he'd been exiled to, living in fear of one day being sent home, where only God knew what would happen to him.

Years, he'd been like that—isolated.

With his eyes fucked enough he couldn't read, and the only conversation he'd had apart from Mario being assholes in the kitchen yelling at him for not moving fast enough, it was no wonder his language had stalled. He had a feeling Vitya could probably drag someone to oblivion with insults he'd picked up, but no one had ever bothered to try and know him before. Not even Mario, really. Not until now.

And he couldn't help but worry that maybe Vitya only felt this way because Mario was the first person to show him true kindness—and it might have been true, but he wanted to trust that Vitya knew himself better than that. He wasn't a child. He was a capable adult who had once been a doctor of philosophy. The mind was a tricky place, but Mario also knew that if he tried, if he let himself soften, he could be the partner Vitya deserved.

They couldn't be out at work, though. Mario only had so much pull with his bosses, and he didn't want to put Vitya at risk. That alone was enough to set him off, and he pushed away from his desk, grabbing his keys on the way out of his office.

Vitya was nowhere to be found, which was probably for the best since he needed some time to get his head in order. Vitya deserved to be better than someone's dirty little secret, but Mario could hardly change immigration laws or—well, shit, he couldn't even begin to understand the dynamics of Vitya's move to the U.S. How could he fix it, how could he keep him safe without compromising this new, growing thing between them?

Mario found himself wandering the main street, hovering near the doorway to Masala as he contemplated a latte. Inside, he saw the café was mostly empty, though through the fogged windows he could see a couple of bodies covered in tattoos, and he knew if anyone could help him with advice, it would be whoever was inside.

He pushed the door open without letting himself overthink it, and he couldn't help his smile when Miguel and Derek smiled at him from their table.

"Yo," Derek said, waving at him. "What's up, man?"

"Coffee," Mario told him with a half-laugh. There was a young kid who looked barely out of high school behind the counter, staring at him with some nerves, which probably meant it was his first day. Mario went easy on him and ordered a café au lait, then strolled over to the table as he waited.

"Long day?"

"I fucking hate Christmas," Mario groaned, and that much was true. "This weekend should be erased from history."

Derek rolled his eyes. "You sound like Basil. I literally can't walk through a single store without him jumping up on his soapbox of cultural erasure. The other day we were in that little home goods place over on Baker and the freeway. They had this little Chanukah display set up, and I swear he almost had a rage stroke."

Mario lifted a brow. "Because they had Chanukah decorations?"

"Because they had *one single stand* of Chanukah décor in a sea of Christmas vomit—his words," Derek said, and he signed them for good measure.

Mario couldn't help his laugh, and he was still chuckling when the kid brought over his drink. "Are you two at least coming to my Chanukah dinner tomorrow?"

Derek looked over at Miguel, then back at him. "Chanukah dinner? I thought you guys did that big Christmas thing up at the hotel."

Mario rolled his eyes and sank into the free side of the booth. "God, my boss is such an asshole sometimes." He took a long drink, then sighed out his frustration. "I wanted to do something more this year, but she gave me such shit about how there's such a small Jewish population in the town, there would be no point in having a Chanukah dinner. Then she went on and on about how it was a minor holiday and not worth celebrating." He dragged a hand down his face. "It doesn't surprise me at all she did like zero advertising for it."

"Count us in," Miguel piped up.

Mario glanced over at him, at the little smirk on his face, and he couldn't help his own grin. He didn't know Miguel well—but what he did know, he liked. He was a huge dude—good looking in the strangest way with his scarred face, shorn head, and massive shoulders. Rumor had it he was an ex-biker, but Mario hadn't ever felt brave enough to ask about his past.

"Dude, you're not Jewish, are you?" Derek asked Miguel.

"No. But like, it's bullshit they're trying to pull the percentage card," Miguel retorted, then looked back at Mario. "Can my fiancé and I go?"

Mario laughed, but it wasn't unkind. "Fuck yeah you

can go. Bring as many people as you can. It's kind of pricey but…"

"Put us down for," Derek stopped and counted silently, his lips moving through the numbers, "Sixteen adults and like nine kids?"

Mario's eyes widened. "Are you sure. That's…"

"Basil is going to shit bricks when he realizes he didn't know about this. Like, first of all, he hates cooking, but second of all, I think it might be the first time anyone around here has done something mainstream for his holiday."

Mario felt a rush of elation, then panic because it was even more important now that this go off without a hitch. He closed his eyes for a second, picturing Vitya standing behind him, guiding his hands through the challah. He wanted Vitya to have part of it too—to be able to celebrate and not work himself into exhaustion during his own holiday.

"You okay?"

Mario blinked his eyes open and looked over at Miguel who was wearing a mask of concern. "Yeah, sorry. It's been a long day. Um." He bit his lip, glancing at Derek. "Do you guys do presents? I mean, do you get your husband presents?"

"Yeah," Derek said, and gave him a small grin. "I mean, he does Christmas stuff with me too—blended house and all that shit. But yeah, I usually get him and the kids something small for each night. He's an easy guy to please, though."

Mario worried his bottom lip between his teeth, then dug his phone out to send a text off to his sous.

Mario: Hold down the fort until I get back. Few errands to take care of. But this Chanukah dinner needs to be perfect—just got a rush of reservations. Heard?

Cash: Heard.

He tucked his phone away, then looked back up at Derek and Miguel. "I think I might be in trouble. I'm…having a thing. With a guy. And I think now I need to shop."

Derek looked troubled, but Miguel eclipsed that with his grin. "You've come to the right person, my friend. I love shopping."

Derek laughed. "I gotta get back to work. I have clients until six. But trust me, with this dude," he gave Miguel's shoulder a pat, "you're in good hands."

Mario let out a short breath. "You may be saving my life."

Mario handed over his credit card for the last purchase, looking dubiously at the small stack of winter mittens being shoved into the bag. It felt like both over-kill and not enough, and he wondered if Vitya would end up feeling shitty because he couldn't reciprocate in the same way.

Mario had no way of explaining to him that the only gift he wanted was Vitya staying in his life without coming across like an asshole, but he also couldn't *not* get him something.

"I should do something for the house," he said, dragging his finger across the small Chanukah display at the store. There wasn't much, a little talking moose, some lights, a couple of cheap looking menorahs, and candles. "Would that be stupid? I'm not Jewish. Hell, I barely celebrate my own holiday, you know?"

Miguel shrugged, leaning his back against the counter, and he crossed his arms, tucking his stump under his armpit. "I think he'd appreciate the gesture."

"Maybe," Mario breathed out. He looked back at the small pile of gifts and his cheeks went a little warm. "I feel like an ass. He's not like...he's not in the position to do anything for me. Hell, we fell into this whole thing by accident, and..." Mario swallowed thickly. "I'm his boss. Part of me is like, give him a pay raise, you know? But that would be fucked up. So how do I even do this?"

Miguel's lips twitched into a half grin and he cocked his head to the side. "You've got it bad."

With a groan, Mario turned back to the display and snatched a package with garishly colored plastic dreidels from the rack—the last one, half-hidden behind the stuffed moose. "I do. I've never done anything like this before. I've never...*fuck*. I've never, like, been in love."

"I have. And it's both amazing and the worst thing you can go through." Miguel's voice was soft and a little pained. "I also think I kind of get it. My fiancé, Amit." He stopped and chuckled like there was an inside joke. "My situation was just about as fucked as your guy's. I mean, Amit wasn't my boss—that one is kind of special."

"Please don't," Mario begged.

Miguel held up his hand in surrender, then pushed off the counter and walked forward. "I had the most bizarre year of my life a couple years back. I went on my journey for this shop in Florida I was working at, and I get here and find myself falling in love with this...," he laughed a bit, like he couldn't find the words. "He's this amazing man and he has no business loving someone as fucked up as I am. But he does. There was so much bullshit that happened when it started though. I had family drama and I had such a low opinion of myself, I didn't think it would ever work. I lashed out at him, and I made it hard for him to love me, but he did anyway. And here we are. If it feels like that, it's worth fighting for, man."

"It does," Mario said, then hesitated. "I think it does. I wish I had something to compare it to."

"When I'm with Amit," Miguel told him, stepping even closer, "it feels like I can breathe again. And I didn't even realize I was having trouble until I have him in my arms."

"Yeah," Mario breathed out. He felt settled in ways he never expected to, and he wasn't quite sure how to handle it. Rubbing a hand down the center of his sternum, he remembered the way Vitya had touched him, the way his fingers had traced his scars, how they'd gripped his ribs like he never wanted to let go.

Mario had never felt like that before. Ever.

"Yep," Miguel said, and Mario looked at him, realizing Miguel was reading the look on his face. "It's like that."

"So, does that mean I get to blame you if he throws all this shit at my face and says he never wants to see me again?"

Miguel grinned wider. "If it helps you take that first step, man, then go for it. I'll happily shoulder the blame if it means you might get your happily ever after."

"That's…wow. That's awful."

Miguel shrugged. "That's also love, my friend, so get used to it."

Chapter 12

Vitya couldn't help but be grateful for the reprieve from his messy thoughts with the chaos of the holiday season. He was put with the banquet team in order to help set up for the Chanukah dinner, and then he'd be staying late to assist for the Christmas prep in the lounge. He tried not to think about how it was the first night, about how he wouldn't be lighting any candles on time, how a prayer would go unsaid apart from in his thoughts as he worked.

And it had been like that every year, it had been like that since he could remember. It was hard to feel better now that he was safe, but as he stared around the ballroom at the massively lit tree, at the lights draped across windows like electric icicles, at the baubles and garlands and tinsel—it was hard not to feel a pang of resentment for being so easy to forget.

Himself, his people, his culture, his very existence. It wasn't as hard when he had a good life. When he was a man of some standing, a man with a job and a home and a reputation. Now he was less than a nobody, without a penny to his name, and no real place to call his own. It was just a harder pill to swallow.

Even as he thought about Mario's arms, the way he held him until he slept, the way that Mario had made love to him and made his body sing. It felt like so much he wasn't sure he deserved, and he was terrified to want now that he could just reach out for him.

Not having was painful, but losing Mario now that they had crossed that line would destroy him.

It was around lunch when Vitya decided to go searching for his wayward chef, but his office door was closed and locked, and no one had seen him for most of the morning. He eventually found Cash, the sous chef, working on the night's special, and he gave Vitya an annoyed look when Vitya tapped his shoulder.

"You have seen Chef today?"

Cash rolled his eyes. "He's out for the afternoon."

"...out?" Vitya repeated.

Cash set down his knife and gave him a flat look. "He doesn't need you bothering him at a time like this. So, can you please just fuck off and go wash a dish or something? I know there's a ton of shit to get done around here and I'm not interested in this weekend going to hell because you made yourself his little pet."

Vitya took a step back in shock, his stomach twisting with fear and humiliation. "I'm not," he started, but Cash had turned back to his work, unceremoniously dismissing Vitya from the conversation.

Swallowing thickly, he rushed around the corner to the dish pit to find stacks of pots and pans waiting for him, and it was with trembling fingers that he got to work. He was a fool to try and cross that line here—a fool for thinking Mario would want to openly acknowledge knowing him at all, even as his employee.

It was proof that their little bubble at home—where they clung to each other like they needed to touch in order to breathe—would only last that little while. They were from two different worlds, and always would be. Hoping for more would only lead him to disappointment and regret, and he'd rather live with the memory of what he had, than quietly pining for what he didn't.

Mario did find him, though, hours later before the dinner shift was about to begin. Vitya had steadfastly avoided the kitchen for most of the day, and ended his shift leaning against the wall, his body aching with fatigue as he stirred a spoon through his tepid soup. He was nearly asleep when a hand touched his shoulder, and he jolted upright, blinking into a too-familiar face.

Mario was smiling gently down at him, but there was concern in his eyes when he reached over and pulled a chair up to the table. "Hey. I was looking for you today."

Vitya gave a shrug, tamping down on just how good it felt to see Mario again—how right it felt for Mario's hand to rest on his shoulder. "Was busy."

"Yeah I…I know. I didn't want to interrupt you or anything. Cash said you had a lot going on." Evidently, Vitya had grown less competent at hiding his frustration, because Mario instantly read his expression and leaned in. "What happened?"

Vitya wave him off. "Is nothing. Busy today—with holiday."

"Cash was being a dick again, wasn't he?" Mario pressed, and Vitya didn't answer, biting the inside of his cheek to keep quiet. After a moment, Mario rolled his eyes and sat back, dragging one hand down his face. "I need to get better staff. Fuck I…I'm sorry. Whatever he did, I'm sorry."

Vitya shook his head, swallowing past a lump in his throat. It was damn near impossible to just let things be when Mario insisted on showing compassion where so few had any. He told himself he shouldn't let himself want this—that it would only end in disaster, but Mario made it impossible to walk away.

"Why don't you take the night off," Mario said after a long silence. "It's the first night, and you're exhausted and…"

"No," Vitya bit. "I'm…I'm need money!" His face burned with embarrassment and he turned his head, taking in a shuddering breath. At times like this, he wished he was blind in the bright light as well as dim, because looking at Mario's face made everything feel both impossible and possible all at the same time. It was too damn much. "Is easy for you. Take vacation, take time. Not worry. But I have bills, have rent, need more than this," he waved his hand at the soup. "I'm already working on Shabbat, because I can't miss more."

Mario looked devastated, and Vitya felt a pang of guilt over it, but he wasn't sorry. He wasn't sorry, because someone like Mario wouldn't ever really understand how much it took just to *exist*. He didn't get that the single day he missed at work could set him back more than he could catch up on. It was a luxury he hadn't possessed in far too many years. Not since before his hair started greying at the temples, or he started getting lines in the corners of his eyes.

He didn't dare look over again, but when Mario touched his hand, he couldn't make himself pull back. "Come to my office later. I'm…I'm sorry. I'm being a totally inconsiderate dickhead and I didn't mean to be. I have something for you, and I want to make it up to you. Okay?"

Vitya finally looked over, and the sincerity in Mario's eyes nearly floored him. "Okay. Yes."

Mario sighed out his relief, squeezing Vitya's hand just once before pulling back. "And please eat something more than soup if you're working a double. You need to keep up your energy." With that, he winked, and Vitya's stomach twisted with want in spite of every conflicted feeling he was having. The man had a way of breaking down any barrier he put up, and it wasn't hard to understand this was a losing battle.

It might destroy him, but it would probably be worth it in the end.

The dinner rush was as bad as ever—worse, in fact, since people were coming in for the holidays. It meant the guests were ruder and more demanding, and it bled into the servers' moods, which bled to the kitchen. The whole of the staff took their frustration out on Vitya, who stayed safely behind his dishwasher, taking the harsh words and abuse they flung at him with a grain of salt.

"You're so fucking slow. God, why the fuck don't they fire you? I need cups now, dipshit!"

"Holy shit, are you blind *and* deaf? Where is my silverware? I'm not going to fuck my tips because you can't get anything done right!"

He closed his eyes against it, kept working, and wished desperately that Mario was around to at least deflect some of it. But Vitya reminded himself he couldn't rely on Mario for that. It wasn't his place. The kitchen ran like any kitchen—a little cold and cruel, but with a sort of comradery that was necessary for this line of work. And most of them weren't in this for life. Most of them were there for a moment, until bigger and better came along. Until they finished their education, and grew up a little, and had careers.

He'd done all that already, and his sharp words had sent him here—a sort of purgatory to live through before death released him.

And then?

There was no telling what came after that.

His religion didn't offer the sanctuary of an intangible savior and streets paved with gold. At best he had an abstract idea of peace after death, and it was the most he could hope for, he supposed.

When the rush calmed down and only the final lingering patrons sat finishing up drinks and desserts, Vitya ventured around from his little soap-soaked cubby and decided to find Mario. It wasn't too late—close to the restaurant closing, but there was still a lot of work to be done. But there was no telling if they'd get downtime after this, so he decided to take the risk.

Two of the bulbs in the hallway were out when he turned the corner, so he braced his hand on the wall and began the slow trek to Mario's office. It was telling that he had the way memorized, telling that he barely needed to guide himself before he was at the door. He liked how familiar the knob felt against his hand, and how he could smell the faint scent of spices and grease which meant Mario was inside.

He took the liberty of not knocking—and in hindsight, maybe that was the real downfall—but he didn't think it was necessary. Not after everything they'd been through. But when he pushed the door open, he was met with a furious glower, and harsher words than he ever expected his lover to direct at him,

Mario was in the middle of the room, shirtless, down to his boxers, and a sweater in one hand. He was turned toward the door, so in the bright lights, Vitya was able to make out his naked chest. It was as muscular as he'd felt it, thin across his middle, freshly shaved hair now growing from his sternum to his pelvis. His nipples were a sort of oval shape, stretched unnaturally, and across the expanse of his skin was a freshly done tattoo that was peeling around some of the edges.

"I," Vitya started, but Mario didn't give him a chance to speak.

"What the fuck do you think you're doing? Are you *stupid*? You can't just walk in here without knocking!"

Vitya took a step back, but stumbled on the door which had half-closed behind him. "Mario—"

"What the fuck are you staring at? *Get the fuck out*!"

Vitya stumbled back, his heart in his throat, cracking into a thousand pieces. The hate in his words was strong enough to gut him, and it was enough to overwhelm him. He didn't care anymore. Not about this job, about this place, about his life. It was nothing anyway. If he was so easy to fling aside, why bother?

He turned and rushed through the back door, his feet sinking into the fresh snow. It would be a cold walk home, but at least he would be away from the one place that had tricked him into giving up his strength. His Delilah, who had cut his hair and made him weak. What an absolute fool he'd been.

But it was fine. He was already blind, but unlike Sampson, he wouldn't wait around to be captured. He would flee. If it sent him back home—so be it. There was nothing left for him here anyway.

Chapter 13

The second the door slammed shut, Mario knew he'd fucked up. Panic had taken over, his words coming from a dark place that had no meaning anymore, but he'd been reacting so viscerally for so long, he couldn't stop them. He would never be able to unsee the heartbreak on Vitya's face, the betrayal as those words pierced him.

They'd been cruel enough to send him running, and now Mario stood rooted to the spot, unsure what to do. His knees buckled after a moment, and he stumbled back into a chair, knocking his clothes to the floor as he sank his face into his hands. His chest burned from the hot water spill, his arm stinging from the burn that had sent him into his office to change in the first place, but none of that mattered in the face of having just chased away the love of his life.

And it was no exaggeration when he said that. No one had ever made him feel the way Vitya did, and *this* was how he repaid him.

His right hand brushed down the center of his chest, skirting around the burn, brushing the edge of his scar where Vitya had touched him the other night. It had been perfect then—more than perfect. And he felt like such an idiot to think that covering his skin with ink would be able to erase those long-standing fears of anyone seeing his chest.

His surgery was years ago—five to be exact. Long weeks he spent bound up and draining, propped up on pillows and in too much pain to lift his hands to his mouth let alone dress himself. But he'd gotten through it, had stayed strong through the pain, and nothing beat that first moment of looking at himself with a flat chest—looking at himself with the body he'd always imagined he should have.

If only that had been enough to erase the years of wrongness, the years of feeling incorrect, the years of people looking at him and knowing they thought he was sick and unnatural. He wasn't afraid of people seeing scars, he was afraid of people seeing someone he wasn't.

He had to fix it. He couldn't lose Vitya over this—couldn't let himself give up one more good thing because the universe created a bunch of assholes who had made him doubt himself. Forcing himself to stand, he slapped the burn salve on his chest and arm, then tugged his sweater over his shoulders, ignoring the sting. His jeans were a little stiff, but they slid on, and he shoved his feet into his running shoes without tying them, grabbing the carefully packed bag he had planned to present to Vitya with far more ceremony than this.

He came to a skidding halt, asking his two line cooks if Vitya had been by, but neither of them had seen him. Either they hadn't paid attention, or he hadn't come that way, and he had a sinking feeling he already knew the answer.

Slipping out the side door, Mario gasped at the cold,

but he didn't let it stop him. His shoelaces dragged through the slush as he shuffled his way around to the parking lot, grateful his car was near the exit. He threw Vitya's gifts into the back, then carefully pulled out onto the street, avoiding the slick patches of ice as he searched.

It was late, and it was snowing a little, but the streets were empty and as cold as he felt without the other man next to him. He would make it up to Vitya—if he could just find him. Panic threatened to overwhelm him, but he wasn't giving up. Worse came to worst, he'd drive to Vitya's place and wait there until he showed up. Come hell or high water, the other man would hear his apology, even if it was thrown back into his face.

Luckily, he didn't need all of those dramatics. Vitya was just walking up his stoop when Mario pulled his car up, and he switched it off before he chased after the other man.

"Please," he gasped, sliding on ice. He managed to catch himself on the stair railing, and when he looked up, Vitya was staring down at him. He wasn't sure the other man could see him in the dimly lit street, but he knew Vitya recognized his voice. "I'm sorry. God, I'm such an asshole. Please just…please let me explain."

"Is okay," Vitya said, and god help him, he sounded sad instead of angry. "I'm understand. My mistake. You can…go home. Is fine."

"No," Mario said. He took the steps until he was one away from Vitya, and he didn't dare touch, even if every instinct told him to take the other man into his arms. "Please, it's not…it was my mistake, and I promise I'll explain if you just let me."

There was a war on Vitya's face, and Mario found he couldn't breathe until Vitya finally nodded his head just the once. "Come inside."

"Okay." He looked helplessly back at his car, at the bag in the back, but there would be time for that later. He followed Vitya up the stone steps, into a frigid hallway that smelled like old cooked fish and cigarettes. He lived on the third floor, his legs burning by the time they got to his landing, and he waited as Vitya opened the door and held it wide.

Mario wasn't quite sure what to expect when he stepped in. He knew Vitya lived poorly, but he didn't realize he lived with virtually nothing. No couch or bed, just blankets lying on a foam mat on the floor beneath the window. There was a small table with a single chair, an immaculately cleaned kitchen, and a door, half cracked, which led to a bathroom.

He felt worse now—worse for flaunting what he had, worse for not bothering to find out the way Vitya was living long before his feelings surfaced. How many of his other employees lived like this? How many suffered because no one bothered to take the time to look?

His stomach twisted, nauseated, and he breathed through it as Vitya shed his coat and rested it along the back of his chair.

"You want to talk?" Vitya asked slowly.

Mario swallowed thickly, then did the only thing he could really think of—he grabbed his sweater by the hem and pulled it off. It fell to the floor with a quiet thud, then he turned back to Vitya and spread his arms. "I'm sorry. Sometimes, when people catch me off guard, it makes me panic. But it wasn't you. Never you, okay? I want you to know all of me. I just didn't even realize it was you at first, and by the time I did, the fear had taken control. And now I..."

"Stop." Vitya's tone was a little cold, but his expression was passive. "I understand this..." He paused, making the face he usually did when he was searching for a word. "Gesture. You making gesture for me. But I'm not see you like this. Too dark."

"Well, *fuck*," Mario breathed out, and Vitya startled him with a laugh.

"Kitchen," Vitya said, and the commanding tone in his voice was impossible to ignore. Mario walked forward, stepping under the harsh light in the ceiling, and Vitya reached over to add the one above the stove.

Mario's entire body hummed with awkwardness at being exposed liked this, but at the same time having Vitya's piercing eyes on him was a strange comfort as he took him in from head to toe. He watched as Vitya's eyes lingered over the ink and scars, then his fingers rose and hovered just above his skin.

"You can touch me," Mario told him, because right then, he'd give Vitya just about anything.

He jolted when Vitya's fingers came down over his sternum where the deer's head rested, and he couldn't help but look down as he watched Vitya trace the outline of his ink with the tip of his finger.

"Beautiful," Vitya murmured. "I could feel it. Not realize it was..."

"Tattoo," Mario filled in for him. "I got it done a little while ago to um...to cover the scars. Or well, to kind of blend them in."

Vitya drew his bottom lip between his teeth and moved his fingers to the scars, then laughed a little as he traced the shape of them. "Like moons. When I touch before, feel like moons."

Mario ducked his head. "Yeah."

"Is different—to see, to feel. Why you want to hide?"

Mario shrugged, daring to look up and face the earnest

expression on Vitya's face. "Before my surgery, I had...they were...big," he gestured toward his right nipple. "I had to bind them, but god—it never worked right. There was always *something* there. And I hated—I *hated*—when people stared at me. It was like, I had this beard, and my voice had dropped a lot, and I looked almost the way I wanted—but not quite. After the surgery, I felt like it was my body. Only...I guess I didn't really get over all those feelings. Not completely."

Vitya nodded, taking a step closer—not quite touching, but close. "Okay. I understand why you feel scared. Why you yell."

Mario shook his head. "Doesn't mean it was right to take that out on you. I just..."

"Panicked," Vitya finished for him, echoing Mario's earlier words. "I forgive."

Mario shook his head. "You don't have to. I didn't come here to win you back. Well, wait. I *did*," he said in a rush, and Vitya chuckled. Mario gave up on all self-control and reached for him, dragging him in so their chests bumped together. "I'm not ready to let you go without a fight."

At that, Vitya looked sad. He reached a hand up and pressed the tips of his fingers to Mario's jaw. "At work, people know I'm...not like you. Not like them. Am different. Less."

"No," Mario breathed out.

"Yes," Vitya countered. "Maybe not here," he touched the space over his own heart, then moved to his temple, "or here. But they believe. And if they know about you and me..."

"I don't care," Mario started to say, then he realized he was yet again focusing on himself without taking into consideration that it put Vitya at risk, not him. The worst he'd suffer is a reprimand at work and mocking from his staff.

Vitya—he could lose everything.

"I'm sorry," Mario breathed out. He tried to step away, but he couldn't bring himself to do it. Losing Vitya now—he wasn't sure he'd ever get over it. His hands dropped to the other man's waist and he clung to him. "I don't want to lose you," he whispered, his voice breaking. "I know I fucked up already, but please..."

Vitya's head bowed and he turned, burying his face against the side of Mario's head. "You have me."

"How do we make this work? Viktor," he said, because he wanted him to know that this was serious, "tell me how to make this work."

Vitya pulled back, swallowing thickly. "I'm finding other job. Is only way."

Mario closed his eyes, but he nodded because Vitya was right. "I know people—I have friends who can help. Friends who will understand why you can't...why things are more complicated for you. It won't be like the resort this time, I swear."

Vitya's face was unreadable for a long moment, then he nodded. "Okay. Okay, we talk to them."

"It doesn't have to be in a restaurant either," Mario went on, rushing far ahead of himself. "It doesn't have to be anything you don't want to do. We can figure it out. Just...say we're okay."

"We okay." Vitya touched his chin, tipping it down, then raised his head and took Mario's mouth in a kiss. It was sweeter and more chaste than any kiss they'd shared before. Vitya's lips were a little cool, but soft, his mouth parting open for just a quick sweep of his tongue before he pulled back. Mario was breathless, like he'd run a mile, and he sagged gently against Vitya's chest.

"Is cold," Vitya murmured against the top of his head. "Put on shirt, yes?"

Mario flushed, rolling his eyes as he eased away from Vitya's grip and went back to the spot he'd dropped his sweater. It felt snug against his skin, a little too warm, too rough against his burns, but he felt lighter than he had in weeks—maybe even months. Vitya had looked at him, had wanted him still, had touched him in every way he could be touched. He was an idiot to be so afraid of this, even if his fear held no real logic. He'd nearly ruined the night, but now there was a future ahead of him he hadn't thought possible, and it was hard not to smile because of that.

"Um. So, I have something for you," Mario said once his clothes were on straight. "Do you mind if I..." He thumbed backward at the door, and Vitya smiled.

"Go. I'm have to light candles—even if late."

"Wait," Mario said, then grinned apologetically. "I mean, please wait? I just...let me..."

He left the room with Vitya's laugh trailing him, and he never felt better.

Chapter 14

Vitya's head was spinning like he was on a carnival ride. How had he gone from the brink of losing everything, to the possibility of something more for his job, and more with the man in his arms. Mario had rushed after him—something Vitya had not expected, then he had bared not only his soul, but his body. He had stood there with arms spread and let Vitya look, touch, hold him and kiss him, and it made everything in the world feel like it could be right again.

It was too easy to accept Mario's words as truth, because they felt honest. Just like the promise of helping him find another job—something that didn't suck the life out of him—felt honest. Maybe nothing would come of it, but Vitya knew he would hate himself if he didn't try.

He was so far from the philosopher he'd once been, and he couldn't help but wonder if those men—all of them his idols, all of them with a privilege he hadn't seen since his twenties—would have believed the same things if they had experienced life like he had.

If they had been thrown out of their home without

hope, identity, or a future, would they have held fast to their beliefs?

He wondered if maybe he was just weak, but at this moment in time, he didn't care. He wished for a moment he had Shabbat candles—if there was ever a time he needed prayer, it was then.

As he waited for Mario to return, he walked to the window where he had a stack of tealight candles resting in a row. It wasn't anything like Chanukah of years' past—of his mother's intricate chanukiah with the twisting branches like a tree surrounding one single trunk that held the one that would light them all. It had been passed down for generations, Hebrew carved along the sides in prayer and worship.

He had never been a firm believer, but he had always loved holidays that represented miracles. In his recent past, the thought of miracles made him feel bitter and angry—because where was his? Now, he supposed, the universe—or maybe God—was just waiting for him to be patient and stay brave.

Had he done that?

He wasn't quite sure.

His fingers brushed over the lighter resting in the crook of the sill, one he'd taken from a chef who had discarded it for not working properly, but it was enough to do what he needed. The night's blessing rested on the back of his tongue, waiting to be sung, but Mario asked him to wait. So, he waited.

He wouldn't be able to see much in the dark, but he would be able to see the glow of the flames. They would illuminate the night—tonight in a pair—the way that Mario had illuminated his life. Only with Mario, he could reach out and touch him without being burnt.

At the sound of the door, Vitya spun, watching the

blurry form that was Mario take better shape as he got closer. He had something in his hands—a paper bag by the sound, and he bent over to set it at his feet.

"So, I was with a friend today. Uh. His name is Miguel —I might have mentioned him before. We met when I was getting some tattoo work done. He works with the guys who own the tattoo shop. Anyway, not important," Mario said, and Vitya laughed quietly at his nervous rambling. "I wanted to do something special for you. I've been so focused on this whole dinner event, but I need you to know that even if it's just some minor holiday—it's important. You're important."

Vitya's throat got tight. "It's okay, Mario, I'm…"

Mario reached out and grabbed Vitya's hand, pushing something into it. A package, wrapped in wrinkled paper. "But open that later. I also, uh…there was this menorah, and it was really pretty." He bent down again, and when he came up, Vitya could just make out a silver chanukiah that was shaped like a bit of driftwood, with holes across the top. "I wasn't sure if this was okay, but it was just…it was cool, and different. If it's totally offensive…"

"Thank you," Vitya told him, interrupting his flow of words. He reached out, not taking it, just letting his fingers brush over the cool metal.

"Everything I read about said you should light the candles at sunset—which I fucked up for you, and I'm sorry about that. I was trying to make time at work—I was hoping we could just do it in the office, but it got so busy and…"

"I think," Vitya said, taking the chanukiah from his hands and placing it where the tea light candles had stood, "God understand. Work is busy, life—busy. We can't control, you know?"

"I know," Mario breathed out softly. He pressed the

box of candles into his hand, and Vitya carefully extracted two.

They fit easily in the chanukiah, and he took a moment to look at the blurry shadows of their shapes before he reached for the lighter. "You study, you know how to sing it?"

Mario laughed. "Yeah uh…no. But in my defense, I don't even know any real Christmas songs apart from like Jingle Bell Rock."

Vitya wrinkled his nose, loving the way it made Mario laugh harder, the way it made him step up and press against his back. "Then I'm sing. You listen."

Mario wrapped his arms around Vitya's waist and held him tight. "Should I let go?"

Vitya's eyes drifted closed, and he took a long breath, letting it out slowly before he spoke again. "No. Never."

"Okay," Mario whispered, then tightened his grip.

Vitya took a moment to feel the warmth, Mario's grip like a candle flame against him, keeping him protected against the cold. When he could move again, he reached for the lighter, using his other hand to guide him to the wick of the shamash, and he watched as it sparked to life. The flame danced, the only thing he could see, and he carefully brought it across each prong until it hovered over the wax of the first candle.

"*Baruch ata Adonai… eloheinu mulch ha'olam,*" the words fell from his tongue in the sweet melody he'd once heard in his mother's voice, in his sister's. Now, from his own lips, they felt strange, because it had been far too many years since he'd sung his blessing aloud. Mario's arms tightened around him, and Vitya felt each finger like warm wax, digging into his skin. "*…'tzivanu l'had'lik neir shel Chanukah…*"

His head bowed slightly, and his eyes moved to the

window to watch the reflection of the flame in the polished glass. "*...shecheyanu v'kiy'manu v'higyanu lazman hazeh.*"

The melody died with the last of the fading blessing, and he touched the shamash to the wick of the first candle. The second flame flared to life, and he used his free hand to guide the shamash back to its rightful place as the *hanerot halalu* fell from his lips, the melody again filling the silent room as easy as it ever had in his youth.

It felt strange, full in a way he hadn't ever experienced back home as a child. In his youth, he felt more anxious to get it done, to rush through it and eat and go play. He had no time for ceremony or pause. He had no time to appreciate miracles for what they were. Now, an actual miracle held him tight, gripped him through this as he sang the final words and took a step back, taking Mario with him.

"Beautiful," Mario murmured, speaking into the back of his hair.

Vitya laughed quietly and shook his head. "My voice... not so good."

"Perfect," Mario said, still whispering like he was afraid to disturb the quiet. "Everything about you is perfect."

Vitya could spend years debating, years coming up with evidence to prove that Mario's opinion was both incorrect and biased—but maybe he didn't need to. He could say the same for the man standing at his back, who would no doubt give the same arguments—and they wouldn't matter. Not to him, anyway. Because it didn't matter how the rest of the world viewed Mario. Even with his bad eyes, all Vitya could see was perfection.

"Can I kiss you? Is that... would it be disrespectful to kiss you right now?"

Vitya didn't have the words in English to explain that no, it wasn't, and if it were, he wouldn't care. But he had not abandoned his own philosophies about God—about how earthly things were too trivial to matter. And kissing—showing love, making love—he refused to consider that a sin.

Turning in Mario's arms, he let the other man clutch him close, let him draw their mouths together—chaste at first, then desperate and heated. He swallowed down Mario's groans, his little gasps as he put his thigh between Mario's legs and let his lover grind down on him.

"I want you. Please...*god*. I want you."

"Yes," Vitya answered, the easiest answer he'd ever given. He pulled Mario down toward his makeshift bed, hating he couldn't give him more comfort, but Mario didn't seem to mind. He tugged at their clothes with a desperate tremble to his fingers, not stopping—not satisfied—until they were undressed. Vitya found himself pinned beneath his lover, Mario's legs straddling his, the head of his thick cock pressing between Mario's cheeks.

"I want to feel you. God, can we...I have condoms in my wallet if you...if we can..."

"Yes," Vitya said, putting an end to Mario's obvious begging. "Yes. What you want, I give. Always, I give."

Mario's head tipped forward, and Vitya couldn't make out his face in the dim light, but he felt his punched-out breath, felt his lips drag across the corner of his jaw. Luckily, he didn't have to go far, reaching over for his pants. Vitya could hear him fumbling through his wallet, hear the crinkle of foil, and then he was back. His warm hand curled around Vitya's achingly hard dick, stroking up and down until Vitya was fucking up into the circle of his fingers. When Vitya started to shake, Mario removed his hand, only to roll the condom on, then gripped him tight again.

"I want to feel you inside me," Mario told him, dipping

his head low to speak the words right up against Vitya's lips. "Tell me you want it. Tell me you want me."

"I want," Vitya told him, but English failed him, and the words came tumbling freely and in his own tongue. "*I want you. I want to feel you tighten around me, want to feel like I'm leaving a piece of myself behind in you, so we're never apart. I want you to understand how much I need you. I do love you, God help me. I love you.*"

With a soft cry, Mario sank down on him, his hot heat impossibly tight as he pulled Vitya in as deep as he could. He braced himself on the soft foam on either side of Vitya's head, their noses nearly touching, and Vitya could almost see him. In the faint glow of two flickering candle flames, he could almost—*almost*—make out the soft curve of his jaw, and the slope of his nose, and the way his lips curled into a grin.

"Viktor," Mario breathed out, and then Vitya was fucking him in earnest. With a roll of his hips, Mario took him as deep as he could. Vitya lost all semblance of control as he reached up, taking Mario by the hips to guide his own thrusts, then he reached between them with one hand and pressed his thumb to Mario's dick where it was swollen and pulsing. He held it between his thumb and forefinger, letting Mario guide the pace as he stroked him, and he could feel Mario trembling, feel him getting closer.

Vitya was on a razor's edge, his pleasure waiting for him, his balls tight as he wanted to spill. But he drew it out, waiting for Mario to lead him there, stuttering thrusts up to meet his lover's pace until—

"God, god, I'm coming. I'm coming," Mario gasped. His arms lost strength and he toppled forward, slamming their mouths together as Vitya fucked Mario's dick with the heel of his hand, spending his own load into the condom.

It felt like hours before they came down, hours before Vitya could breathe again. He let out a tiny moan as Mario rolled off him, and he carefully removed the condom, tying it off before throwing it near the bin. It likely didn't make it, but he didn't care. He didn't care when he had this man next to him, this man willing to roll over and press against his chest.

"I don't know what you were saying," Mario breathed out, his voice a little hoarse, "but that was hot as shit."

Vitya chuckled, his own voice a bit rough, and he nosed against Mario's cheek before pulling back. It was a night of miracles—the first one, he hoped, of many to come. But this was enough, so he decided to be brave. He touched Mario's face, drawing his gaze up, and he took a fortifying breath. "I say…that want to be with you. For always. Need you, for always. That I love you."

There was dead silence, but before Vitya could even start to let himself panic, Mario pushed onto his elbow, took Vitya by the face, and kissed him. He laughed through it, teeth clashing together—making it sloppy and ugly and so damn perfect, Vitya wanted to cry. "I love you too. Which is insane. I mean, we just…it hasn't even been a week. Isn't this insane?"

Vitya shrugged as he settled back against his pillow, feeling the hard floor beneath the cushion, but for the first time, not hating it. "Maybe. Is okay. I love you, you love me. Chanukah miracle."

Mario snorted as he laid back down, letting his head rest in the crook of Vitya's arms. "I don't know if that's what all those websites I read meant about the miracle of lights, but…I'll take it."

"I see them," Vitya told him, his voice sobered and soft. He dragged his thumb down around Mario's face, loving the feel of his beard, the curve of his jaw, the dip in his chin. "In you, I see them."

Mario kissed him again, and then again, and then once more before letting Vitya hold him tight and drifting off together.

Chapter 15

"…And you can arrange all that?" Mario asked, palming the keys to the front door with coffees in his hands, his phone pressed between his shoulder and ear. The soothing tones of the rabbi eased his stress about doing this Chanukah dinner properly.

"I can. I have a ceremonial chanukiah that I've used for other events, and it won't take me long to set up. As long as we can have access to the hall before noon."

"That's no problem. Thank you, Rabbi. I know this is totally last minute, but this means a lot," Mario told him, leaning against the door.

The older man chuckled. "I'm surprised is all. Normally we don't get asked."

"I know, and I'd like to change that as often as I can. We can talk later. I just…I have some friends who aren't Jewish who'd like to come, and I hope that's alright. I didn't know if it was against, like, protocol, or rules, or something."

"It's more than fine. It's encouraged. We'd love it," Rabbi Cremen told him in a rush. "All are welcome."

It was a nice sentiment, mostly because it felt genuine—it felt like it was without exception instead of all welcome as long as a person followed a rigid set of rules that didn't allow for diversity or free thought. "I'll be in touch. I have to get over to the hotel, but you can always reach me on my cell."

"Thank you, Chef Garcia," the rabbi said.

"It's Mario," he corrected. "I'm looking forward to meeting you."

He ended the call, then set the coffees on the floor by the cushion, careful not to disturb his lover, before moving back to the kitchen where the cinnamon rolls waited. He'd gone out three times—braving the frozen morning before his massive day at work—but none of it fazed him. He woke with a renewed sense of something—maybe holiday spirit, though that didn't sound right. But he was happy, and that was a change he wanted to keep with him and guard jealously.

When he began baking that morning, he kneaded the dough and hummed the melody to the prayer Vitya had sung the night before. His voice was higher, but raspier from his testosterone, and he didn't have the same flow as Vitya, who had been singing it since his youth. But it was a comfort during his quiet time long before Vitya woke, and he realized it was just the start. It was the second night, and there were six more to come—and then hopefully a lifetime. He didn't want to get ahead of himself, but telling Vitya he loved him had been no small thing.

Every time he heard the words repeated in his head—first in Russian, then in broken English—his heart pounded. It had been just like breathing when he said them back, when he clutched Vitya to him and just let himself feel it. Miguel had been right—it *was* like this.

Plating two of the rolls, Mario checked his messages

and saw the last one from Cash confirming that everything was running smoothly, and Mario didn't need to hurry. He hadn't told Cash why, only to alert HR that they would likely be down one dishwasher and needed to schedule another.

Mario felt himself deliciously sore in places he hadn't realized could get sore—which only served to remind him that his sex prior to Vitya had been lacking. Not that he cared anymore. Vitya loved him. Vitya loved him, and he knew Mario felt the same way, and it was okay.

Vitya would have several meetings the following week with Rowan and Soren to discuss immigration status options, and an interview with Elliot, who ran a veterinary clinic and animal shelter, who was looking for an assistant. He also called up Mat, who said he was going to look into free or reduced cost eye care so Vitya could at least have his vision checked and see if there was anything they could do.

It wasn't much, but it was a start. And right then, that was enough.

Mario carefully balanced the plate on one hand as he pulled the curtains back, taking a moment to admire the easy way Vitya slept. His head was resting to the side, lips parted, hands curled into loose fists near his ears. He looked younger then, more at ease, and Mario wanted to see that on him during his waking hours too.

He glanced over at the floor where he'd laid out the to-go coffees he'd darted out for when he grabbed ingredients to cook, and his eyes focused on the poorly wrapped gift resting next to them. Just a set of mittens with leather palms to help keep Vitya's hands cold and dry. They felt like such a pathetic gift now, in the face of what little he had. He should have gotten him stuff for his kitchen, or more bedding, or a damn bed. He wasn't wealthy by any means, but he had enough.

Still, even through all that, he didn't think extravagant gifts would be welcome. Just like him, Vitya only wanted to be loved, and Mario was finally confident enough he could love the other man the way he deserved. Fierce, unrestrained, reckless, and wild. Mario had tough skin, but underneath he was like anyone else, and he planned to leave himself ripped open where his lover was concerned.

With a sigh, he eased back down onto the floor mat, which had gone flat under their weight, and he shifted and nudged at Vitya's legs until his eyes fluttered open. They blinked rapidly, the sun coming through the window, making them light up a rich maple color—a hint of white fog in the middle where his pupils were, and he could make out a faint dusting of freckles across his nose.

"Morning," Mario said once Vitya looked more aware. "I made breakfast."

Vitya wrinkled his nose. "I'm not have food for breakfast."

"I went out and grabbed a couple things to make cinnamon rolls. We left the challah at my place or I would serve you French toast or something."

Vitya's mouth curved into a smile as he pushed himself up to sit, then he looked startled. "Wait. Work…"

"I called Cash and told him to get started without me. I'm taking at least the morning with you," Mario told him firmly.

"But my shift," Vitya started, but Mario reached out and cupped his chin, quieting his words.

"I'm not going to tell you what to do, but if you want to quit right now—then I'll help you until you find something else. Actually, I have a friend looking for an assistant right now at his vet's office…"

"Wait," Vitya said, holding up his hand. "I'm not understand. Vet's office?"

"Animal doctor," Mario told him. He helped Vitya sit up all the way, then passed over the coffee, which his lover took with a happy hum. "He said he can find plenty for you to do where your vision won't be a problem. And it pays well."

Vitya sighed into the cup, not meeting Mario's gaze. "Is…big favor."

"Not really," Mario told him. "You're not some uneducated trust-fund brat living off his mommy and daddy's credit cards. You were a professor, you're a grown adult, and you have job experience. Elliot's a good guy, okay? He'll figure it out until we can find something that you want to do. And it's better than the kitchen, right?"

Vitya hummed, his nail picking at the waxy coating on the side of the cup. Eventually, he nodded, looking up at Mario. "I think…yes."

"He wants to meet with you next week. And in the meantime, I can either help you out here, or you can come stay with me." Mario reached for him again, cupping the back of his neck and toying with a few of his shaggy curls. "It's the holidays, so I wouldn't hate it if you spent them with me. We can light the candles every night, and you can teach me how to sing that blessing, and…we can make new memories."

Vitya licked his lips, his cheeks adorably dusted with a red blush, and he nodded. "Okay."

"I also have a gift for you," Mario said. He set his cup down and started to reach for the gift, but Vitya grabbed his arm to stop him.

"Wait. Is already too much. Holidays, job, soft bed. You take care of me when I'm sick. Now this?"

"I promise," Mario said, carefully pulling away to grab

the present from the floor, "it's nothing big. Just a little something I wanted you to have. Miguel helped me pick out the presents."

Vitya took it with a hesitant tremble to his fingers, and he narrowed his eyes at Mario. "*Presents.* More than one?"

"One per night. I don't even know if that's a thing, but it sounded cute," Mario defended.

Vitya huffed, but he turned the package over in his hands, testing the crinkle of the edges before he tore one open and pulled the tape off. He took an agonizing amount of time to unwrap something so damn small, but eventually he had them in his hands, his fingers roaming over the soft wool and leather.

"To keep your hands warm when I can't be there to hold them," Mario said.

Vitya looked up at him, his eyes shining as he set the mittens down, then took Mario's face between both of his warm hands. "Thank you. I love them."

"I love *you,*" Mario said, like it was the easiest thing in the world. Because really, it was.

Chapter 16

Never in a million years did Vitya imagine he'd be walking into the ballroom at the Fairfield Resort as an invited guest rather than a man behind a dish cart in a dirty apron. His stomach was in knots and it was hard to feel like he belonged there, even if he was dressed for the holiday—his hair freshly washed and lying in soft curls, his face shaved, in suit trousers and the softest button-up shirt Mario had insisted on buying for him.

But he couldn't stomach the thought of being served by people who had openly and relentlessly mocked him. He didn't want to look them in the face, to know that they would go back behind closed doors and laugh, because he'd never be anything more to them.

He almost cancelled. He almost told Mario that he appreciated all the work he'd put into the night, but he just couldn't bring himself to go. Then Mario had walked with him to the lobby and introduced him to a group of men and their spouses, and some of their children, and suddenly it felt—maybe not quite like home, but it felt like a better place than he'd been in far too long.

Wyatt was the first person who truly put him at ease when he wondered if maybe everyone else was being kind out of pity. His soft French allowed Vitya to speak easily in a language which he was fluent, and it guided him into a sort of calm.

"I was overwhelmed too," he said, putting his hand on Vitya's arm. He had his guide dog with him, who sniffed the cuffs of his trousers then settled at their feet. "I came here to get away, and I fully intended on staying inside my little cabin and being alone for the rest of my life. But it didn't go to plan."

Vitya laughed softly. "Mario—is the same. I put my head down and I work hard. He sees me, and he wants me to see him. But I'm…okay, you know? It's good."

"Yes," Wyatt told him with a grin. "They take care of their own here, and that's something they won't let you forget."

Vitya couldn't doubt him. Mario had made it clear most of the people attending that day weren't Jewish at all, but they were there to support their few friends that were —in an excited way, not just trying to pacify their bitterness at their holidays always being swept under the rug and ignored.

It felt…he couldn't describe it.

"Can you see the hall?" Wyatt asked, his voice interrupting Vitya's thoughts. "There's so many lights, but I wasn't sure…"

"I see it," Vitya told him. Not well, he couldn't see it well, but he could see the blue and white glow of the strings of fairy lights on the banisters, across the tables, over the windows. There was a table shrouded in white, and he couldn't make it out from where he stood, but he knew the chanukiah was there waiting to be lit. It had the same overwhelming feel of winter and family and home the way the banquet hall with the massive Christmas trees and hanging baubles did, and that meant everything. "It's beautiful."

Wyatt nodded, squeezing his arm before stepping back, and Vitya noticed a tall man with stark black hair and thick whorls of black tattoos across his arms. He was smiling, reaching for Wyatt who went easily into his touch. "This is Mat, by the way."

Vitya shook his hand, then pulled back, feeling a sudden rush of envy at all the couples around him. He wasn't alone anymore—but he wanted to share this moment with Mario, and he knew it was selfish of him to ask. Not when his lover was doing so damn much for him already.

"Do you need a guide?" Mat asked when the chatter in the room started to indicate that the rabbi had arrived and was getting ready to light the chanukiah. The sky outside had faded to a dusky red in the distance, and it began to fade from the center of his vision.

"I," he started, but then a familiar hand touched his waist.

"He's good." Vitya looked up into Mario's smiling face, took in the scent of him—the sharp spices from the kitchen, oil from the fryer, and beneath all that, his earthy musk Vitya wanted to roll around in. "You want to get up closer so you can see it better?"

There wasn't a huge crowd—some from the local congregation, a few people who were just curious, and all of the ones Mario had managed to round up over just a handful of calls. Vitya had never been prouder to be part of something in his life.

They shuffled toward the front, Mario's touch on him

like a ballast, and they came to a stop a few feet from the table where the rabbi stood. From what Vitya could see, he was younger—a sharp jaw, full lips, dressed more modern than he would have ever seen in Russia. But he liked it—he liked the differences, and the way it felt a little alien.

Closing his eyes, he let himself sink against Mario's chest as his lover wrapped around his backside, arms tightening around his middle to hold him. He felt safe—he felt wanted and protected, and that meant everything. He couldn't understand much of what the rabbi was saying—his words too fast, his English flowing together with a rhythm his brain couldn't make sense of, but he could feel the ripple of interest through the crowd, and he knew the rabbi was telling the story—explaining why they were here.

And he had always loved the Chanukah story—but right now, his own holiday miracle existed, and it was knowing that which made his faith feel stronger than ever.

The strike of the match was almost startling, and he smelled the pungent smoke as the shamash flared to life. He watched the dance of flame across the chanukiah, and then the rabbi began to sing. Along with him—the few in the crowd who knew the blessing—joined their voices with his. Vitya found the words flowing from his own lips, his voice a chorus with the others. Then, against the back of his ear, Mario began to hum along.

Vitya rocked from side to side, the room entirely black save for that one flame—which then became three. The light glinted off the chanukiah, the only thing in the room his eyes could make out, but it was enough.

The man behind him, the people around him, the future ahead. They would do this next year, and the one after, and it would always mean something special to him. There wouldn't be a single year he could forget. Not with

Mario's warm lips pressing a kiss to the back of his ear, or the way Mario's hand found his and squeezed tight to guide him through the dark.

He was home.

He was free, and he was home.

Epilogue

The sign on the yoga studio never failed to make Mario laugh. ***Two Blind Dudes Yoga and Philosophy***. The opportunity had come along in the most unexpected way when a man named Marcel had breezed into town and set up shop right around the corner from Irons and Works. With how busy Mario had been with his own restaurant, he hadn't gotten to know the guy well, but Vitya had come home walking on air—almost literally—when the guy had proposed working together.

"Is like mind-body," Vitya told him, folding his hands together. "He take care of the body, I take care of the mind." His English had improved enough, Mario felt good about the class. He felt good that someone had taken a look at his fiancé and had understood his worth.

He knew Vitya didn't hate working at the vet clinic with Elliot, but he did know that it wasn't his passion. The offer had come at the right time—in the right way, so Vitya took it without feeling like he was being pitied or patronized.

Mario paused in the entryway, taking in the sun-warm

smell of the wooden floors, and he could hear soft music in the background. The studio had been opened now for three months, but with his own restaurant just getting off the ground, he hadn't had a chance to spend time there the way he'd wanted to.

He would, though. What was important to Vitya was important to him, and he wanted to show him that. He made his way down the hall to Vitya's office, pausing in the doorway to find his lover carefully arranging books in the tall shelf. Mario watched him for a moment, the way he stretched, the graceful way his fingers parted spines to make space. God, he loved him—everything about him, even the annoying and the mundane.

He'd never felt so lucky in his life, and the fact that he got to keep this man…

"I know you're staring at me," Vitya told him without turning around.

Mario laughed, rolling his eyes as he stepped into the office, closed the door, then flicked the little lock. The little snick wasn't lost on his lover, who turned his head with a knowing smile. He waited for Mario to get closer, then dragged him by the front of his shirt, into a heated kiss.

"Hey," Mario said when he pulled back. "Miss me?"

"All day," Vitya told him. He backed up to brace his ass on his desk, pushing aside a thick book filled with the braille he'd been working on since the doctors told him that his cataracts could be fixed, but the glaucoma they'd been masking couldn't. They could stay the vision loss, but not recover it, and Vitya had taken it all with a grace Mario wasn't sure he'd ever possess. "You missing me?"

"Always," Mario told him. He wrapped his arms around Vitya, slotting between his legs, then dragged his hands down to his ass. "I don't have too long. I have to get back for the dinner rush, but I needed to be with you for a bit."

That was also no lie. Their new jobs took a toll on their personal time, and even though they always went to bed together, he felt like a piece of him was missing when he went too long without Vitya in his arms.

"Kiss me, then," Vitya said. "I have class in fifteen minutes. Enough time to make you feel good."

"Actually," Mario said, and his hand drifted to the zipper on Vitya's trousers. "I was hoping you'd let me. Last night I had a dream that I sucked you off at your desk and I'd really like to make that a thing."

Vitya groaned, but he let Mario drag him up by his shirt, then seat him in the chair before falling to his knees. It didn't take long to draw Vitya out from the slit in his boxers, and he could tell from the way he throbbed, the way he leaked precome in a steady stream, he was ready. He wouldn't last long, and it was heady that he still had this effect on his lover even after being together for two years.

"Please," Vitya said when Mario leaned down to lick a stripe from base to tip. At the sound of his begging words, Mario sucked the head into his mouth, feeling it come free of his foreskin. The taste was like nothing else, no real way to describe it, but god, he craved it. He craved everything about this man. From the way he whispered Mario's name, to the way he touched him and made his body sing. From the way he felt deep inside Mario, or the way he felt beneath him when Mario fucked him into the bed.

It was everything.

There was no other word for it.

Gripping the tops of Vitya's thighs, he sank down deep, feeling the head of Vitya's cock brush the back of his throat. He choked just a bit, pulling back with a hard suck, then shoved his hand into Vitya's boxers to grab his balls. By now, he knew Vitya's body like his own—exactly where to touch, how hard to pull, how gentle to squeeze.

It took less than a minute before Vitya was fucking his face, and thirty seconds after that before he was coming with a soft cry, his hips stuttering up as Mario milked every last drop. He swiped his mouth with the back of his hand before sitting up, then let Vitya gather him close on his lap, holding his face as they kissed slow, languid, and hot.

"Thank you. You want me to…" Vitya asked, palming his crotch.

Mario was wearing his packer, so he didn't feel much beyond pressure, but he liked it anyway. He liked that Vitya fondled all the parts of him—ones that stayed, ones that could get put away at the end of the night. He breathed out a sigh, then kissed under his ear. "I'm good. I really do have to get back, but I wanted to make sure nothing came up for tomorrow."

It was the first night of Chanukah, and a sort of anniversary for them. It wasn't the night they fell in love, but it was the night they let themselves accept the miracle that brought them together. Borne of pain and suffering—and it was all very Jewish, Vitya insisted, which always made Mario laugh.

But it was a testament to his own patience, and their combined endurance. They'd come from dark places to find each other, a flickering candle flame in the distance—but all they had to do was reach out to touch the light. Mario wouldn't have traded it for the world—not for anything the universe could give him.

"I think," he started to say, but a soft *murr* from the corner of the room interrupted him, and Mario turned his head to see the small, pale orange cat curled up on one of the shelves. "Oh my god, was he here the whole time? He's always watching us. He's such a pervert."

Vitya chuckled, then broke away from Mario, pushing him back so he could stand. Taking a step from the chair, he sank into a crouch and wriggled his fingers. "Snuggle… you want some love? Come, I give."

Mario rolled his eyes as the arrogant little shit stretched, his paws spreading to reveal sharp claws before hopping down. He gave Mario a look that said, '*He will always love me just a little more than you*,' as he curled around Vitya's ankles, his head bumping into Vitya's extended fingers. "I hate that cat."

Vitya scoffed under his breath, scooping Snuggle from the floor and cradling him close. "Just jealous he has more fur, get more pets."

Mario recalled the day the little orange shit strolled into the kitchen. Half the staff chased it down, and eventually he found it cowering under the desk in his office. He took the damn thing home with the intent of sending it to work with Vitya the next day to place into Elliot's shelter, but somehow, the little beast crawled under Vitya's skin. Before Mario had realized it was happening, they had a cat.

Snuggle—which would forever make him roll his eyes.

"You're a philosopher, with a *doctorate*, and you want to name him *Snuggle*?"

"Is snuggly," Vitya had argued, stroking the cat under the chin.

Mario had glowered at the purring thing in Vitya's arms—the arms that should have been around him, the little thief. "Shouldn't you call him like, I don't know, Wittgenstein or Nietzsche, or…hell, Descartes?"

If looks could kill… "He not so ordinary as those

men." He stroked the cat again and nuzzled the top of his head with his nose. "Snuggle face. I'm call him…Snuggle."

It was a fight Mario had never won.

With a sigh, he urged Vitya to stand so he could press one last kiss to his fiancé's lips. They walked to the door together, both stepping into a patch of fading afternoon sun which belied how cold it was outside that late November. Vitya dropped Snuggle back to the ground, their hands tangling together, and Mario looked down at the cat before staring back up into his lover's face. Vitya's eyes were closed, his head tipped back slightly. He looked ethereal, basking in the soft glow of afternoon light, and Mario knew that this was forever.

Come hell or high water, come any disaster, this was it.

The End

Subscribe to my newsletter, or for those of you already subscribed, click here for a free bonus chapter of To Touch the Light and get a first glimpse at Soren and Kane from the future book, Renegades: Book One of Breaking the Rules—and Irons and Works spin-off.

Acknowledgments

Thank you to my sensitivity readers. To Luke, my best friend without whom Mario would be a shell of a man instead of the character brought to life on the page. To Paul Castle for your insights on living with visual impairment and in general for being an amazing person and one of my favorite artists. To Lolly for life experience that I can't regret, no matter what became of us. To Kate, whose three sentences in an instant message birthed this story, who talked me through it, and loved both Mario and Vitya as much as they deserve. To Emo, whose love for these boys and whose sage advice kept me sane through this process. To Katy, my editor and platonic soulmate—I love you. To my readers, because I wouldn't be here without you.

Coming Soon

January, 2020

Breaking the Rules, Book One: Renegades

Soren Green is a good man. An ex-MMA fighter, single father, and a lawyer helping to better the lives of LGBT teens. But his life isn't as simple as it seems, and things get turned a little upside down when he stumbles on a troubled man on the side of the road, making his way through a snowstorm. Soren knows one of his biggest problems is his bleeding heart, but how can he turn away when he was once that man out in the cold?

Kane Winters once had it easy. Rich parents, silver spoon, everything at his disposal. But Kane was never a lucky man, and nothing is proof of that more than his abusive boyfriend dying in a freak accident, and his uncontrollable anger sending him into a tailspin. He returned to Fairfield with a chip on his shoulder, felony on his record, and no hope of recovering himself as the man he once was. Kane was certain that he was condemned to this life

—cold, alone, and unloved. Then, in the middle of a storm, a stranger pulls over to offer him a ride. Kane took a blind leap once, and it almost destroyed his life, but he's not so sure the bald man with the walking cane and kind eyes would be anything like his ex.

Will the two men figure out a way to make it work, or will their pasts continue to lead them to a future without hope?

Also by E.M. Lindsey

Works by E.M. Lindsey

Baum's Boxing:

Book One: Below the Belt

Book Two: Fortune and Fate

Book Three: Fringe Contender

Irons and Works:

Book One: Free Hand

Book Two: Blank Canvas

Book Three: American Traditional

Book Four: Bio-Mechanical

Book Five: Stick-And-Poke

Book Six: Scarification

Irons and Works Novellas:

Last Minute Walk-In

OMNI Corp:

Lesser Things

Magnum Opus Series:

Verismo

Tremolo

Serenata

Stand-Alone Novels:

Like Water Catching Fire

Forget-Me-Not

Endless Forever

About the Author

E.M. Lindsey currently lives in Gainesville, Florida with her family. In what precious little time she has to herself, she reads gay romances and binges GBBO, the Chilling Adventures of Sabrina, and terrible 80s and 90s romcoms on Netflix.

Find E.M. Lindsey's website at elainelindsey.com for news, sales, and updates. Join E.M. Lindsey in her Facebook group Lindsey's Liaison for chances at ARCs, cover reveals, sneak peeks, and giveaways.

To support people like the characters in these books, please consider donating to the following charities:

US:

National Association for the Deaf
ChildHelp
PTSD USA

UK:

British Deaf Association
NAPAC
PTSD UK

Printed in the USA
CPSIA information can be obtained
at www.ICGtesting.com
LVHW040813040124
767971LV00004B/1005